Phil,
Best Wishes
Daniel L.

Le Blanc'd

By

Daniel Lechner

TATE PUBLISHING
AND **ENTERPRISES**, LLC

Published by Tate Publishing & Enterprises, LLC
127 E. Trade Center Terrace | Mustang, Oklahoma 73064 USA
1.888.361.9473 | www.tatepublishing.com

Tate Publishing is committed to excellence in the publishing industry. The company reflects the philosophy established by the founders, based on Psalm 68:11,
"The Lord gave the word and great was the company of those who published it."

Published in the United States of America

ISBN: 978-1-62147-617-7
1. Fiction / General
2. Fiction / Mystery & Detective / General
12.06.04

PART ONE

Chapter One

"Fasset, get in here . . . now!"

Preston Daley, a six foot, 60-year old man of some girth, retreats from his office doorway, and begins briskly pacing back and forth in front of his desk. He is preoccupied. From his glass-windowed office, located in the center of a large news gathering room, Preston Daley is always visible to his employees. They can see something is not right today as he overlooks his empire; this medieval King is in his castle, viewing his village below. This is his world. He is the King. No one can dispute the King!

A hesitant Basil Fasset meekly enters his office.

"Yes sir, Mr. Daley?"

Preston Daley tosses, or more accurately throws, some papers in front of Fasset. Loud shouting begins!

"Look at these numbers! This is the end, Fasset! I can't have any more of this. These numbers are totally unacceptable. You'll have to get our circulation up immediately, Fasset, or I'll get someone in here who can. Do we understand each other on this?"

In the news room, most Statesman employees pretend to

be focused on other work projects, but in reality it is hard for them not to be somewhat interested in the meeting now taking place before them, especially after listening to Mr. Daley's opening outburst. They can hear nothing inside Mr. Daley's office, but body language tells the story!

A shaking Basil Fasset, the balding, frail circulation manager of the Preston Daley owned Washington States- man newspaper, picks up the strewn papers from the floor, quickly organizes them, and slowly begins to scan the numbers. He takes his time. What he is viewing is not news to him. Circulation is way down. He knows it. Cir- culation has been dropping steadily for years, but today the numbers reflect a level below the critical threshold of 100,000 newspapers per day. This event will eventually spell disaster for the Statesman!

Basil Fasset knows all about large fixed-cost businesses . . . a revenue drop below a critical threshold is a sign big trouble is coming. At the Statesman, a further 5% drop in revenue won't mean a 5% drop in earnings; it will mean no earnings at all, because the last 5% was the profit, the dol- lars which remained after all fixed expenses were account- ed for. With these numbers today, the Washington States- man has reached its critical point.

A puzzled Fasset looks directly at Mr. Daley wondering . . . why are you now holding me accountable for all this? I'm just the circulation manager. I'm doing the best job anyone can. What is happening is way beyond my control. This trend is not new; it's been going on for some time. Much more seems to be at play here, much more than any failings on my part.

This reeling circulation manager has done his utmost during his entire career of 37 most difficult years, trying to please Mr. Daley and trying to make sure the paper is pro- duced in a first-rate condition and delivered each day. He has given his all to this newspaper, but Mr. Daley doesn't appreciate any of that now. He only threatens and scolds him today.

Preston Daley, as the King, is a bully. He routinely talks in condescending tones to all his employees, and over the years has buried anyone who has dared to threaten his authority. This behavioral trait has extended not only to employees, but also to outsiders who have tried to get in his way, both professionally and personally. This man, Preston Daley, has few friends. His total life is the Statesman, and guiding it single handedly is his mission!

Few can argue with his success. The Statesman, being the number two newspaper behind a dominant Washington Ledger, is always in a most vulnerable position, but somehow has managed to survive over the years with this third generation Daley at its helm. Somehow Preston Daley has managed to guide the Statesman safely thru dangerous journalistic seas. Being number two in any field is perilous, but still the Statesman, with Preston Daley as its leader, has flourished; that is, it has flourished until the present time. Something is different today. A once successful business model for the Statesman is slowly crumbling; the finely tuned machine father Ward Daley created is sputtering. This surely hasn't happen overnight.

What possibly could have caused such a reversal to unfold? No one in management at the newspaper seems to have any idea, but a clue might be found in the fact that monumental changes in technology have occurred in the past 10 years. The Internet has changed everything! All media has been affected by this change, and not just the newspaper business. With this new Internet, old ways quickly go by the wayside; new patterns of distribution emerge at a heady pace. Instant gratification is possible with the new. Countless varieties of news stories are possible from anywhere on earth, instantly. Cost of production is miniscule.

The Statesman has awakened in this new world unable to compete on the same playing field. Its product, a mid-twentieth century warm-up, suffers from years of effort spent trying to contain escalating costs of production and distribution, and has morphed into a cute "sameness" with all other newspapers. Nothing separates the Statesman from its competition, or defines its uniqueness anymore. Former loyal readers seem to have discovered this fact, and are no longer willing to pay a high price for such journalistic blandness. Other options are available to them today; gradually these readers are embracing the new electronic media. This is the frightening state of affairs facing Preston Daley today.

"Fasset, I want new ideas. I want fresh ideas. I want ideas that will work. I don't want any retreads. I don't want any more excuses. I want something on my desk Monday morning! Do whatever it takes. This will be your defining moment, Fasset. Get it done, or get out!"

A totally battered Fasset exits Mr. Daley's office, shuffles toward his desk, sits down, and just stares into his computer screen. It is Wednesday afternoon. He has only 4 days to do the impossible. He continues to slouch over his computer screen, in a very poor effort trying to make an appearance of working, but his simple charade is not fooling any of his immediate co-workers for one moment. They know the signs of a stunned man. They can sense here is a completely whipped man. Basil Fasset is a beaten man. No one ever emerges from a dual with Mr. Daley intact.

Chapter Two

Georgetown, located in the northwestern portion of our nation's capitol, serves as the modern ancestral home of the Daley family. Here Preston Daley and his wife Bonnie reside in a magnificent 4-story townhouse, built in 1887 by great grandfather Casey Daley. That year, incidentally, also happens to mark the year of the founding of the Statesman. The Daley family easily qualifies as "old residents" of Georgetown.

Great grandfather Casey Daley was an interesting fellow, an adventurer, a sea captain, a man never afraid of a challenge, and a man willing to risk all if he found a potential reward great enough. The American Civil War provided just the opportunity, and the family's great wealth was accumulated during this time period via a blockade-running venture for the Southern States. Dangerous work, but exorbitant profits if you can do it!

After the war, Casey settled down to a slower life of commerce, and then staked Grandfather Donnell with the money to found the Statesman. This new venture slowly prospered as a conservative newspaper under Donnell's nurturing eye, but things really boomed under Preston's Father, Ward's, creative guidance during the 1920's, to become the number two publication in the Capitol. Ward was its true creative genius, the man with the vision and the plan to allow the Statesman to leapfrog all other newspapers except the Ledger. Preston took control in 1969, with a heavy hand and a firm grip, and a mission to preserve what Ward had created. It comes as no surprise that the same business model remains in place today.

It is Wednesday evening, 7:28 p.m. A black limousine pulls up to the front door of the Daley townhouse to unload its occupant. Tonight could be any Wednesday evening of the year, in any season, for it is always the same on this particular evening. Preston Daley emerges from the back seat of the parked limousine, and approaches the front door of his townhouse. The front door opens, Bonnie greats him with the obligatory peck on the cheek, then hands him a scotch and soda; the door closes and the two enter the foyer together. Bonnie is Mrs. Daley, the perky brunette socialite wife of Preston, some 12 years his junior.

"Was it a tough day today, my dear? You seem preoccupied!"

"Let's just say the day is over."

Such a short conversation, always such a short conversation! Every Wednesday evening is the same. Not a further word is spoken as the couple crosses the foyer, then the Great Room, on their way to the library.

The foyer of the Daley townhouse opens onto the main room of the first floor, the Great Room, which is a giant gathering space, almost the size of a ball room. It is here that formal entertaining, so important to the success of the newspaper, has occurred for three generations. This room is a masterpiece of architectural workmanship, with stunning solid walnut-paneled walls and cornices throughout, but the real jewel of the room is the Daley art collection, a collection consisting of original pieces accumulated over a one hundred year time span. On the street side of the room a very impressive circular stairway ascends over the foyer to the second floor, where visitors may gaze down upon the opulence greeting them from below. Certainly, time has stood still in this townhouse for over 100 years!

In the library, Mr. and Mrs. Daley sit down on identical, older, wing-tipped leather chairs in front of a fireplace. Maxwell, their servant, always has a fire waiting. It is now that some semblance of conversation begins, but usually only about topics of concern to Bonnie. Preston Daley never shares office news with his wife.

"Don't forget, we will be meeting with our new neighbor on Sunday afternoon. Count Le Blanc has invited us for cocktails and wine at 3:00 p.m."

"Uh...huh . . . yes, I haven't forgotten."

Preston Daley is in no mood for conversation at the moment. He still focuses on the newspaper circulation numbers and what to do about Fasset. With his second scotch and soda, he softens somewhat, and becomes more sociable.

"Darling, was your shopping trip today fruitful?"

Every Wednesday Bonnie Daley spends the day at Gala's Department Store with her close friend Sheila, the wife of Senator Stratum. They pamper themselves initially with a salon appointment, then lunch in the 9th floor restaurant, and finally leisurely walk thru each of the many departments, trying to find just the perfect item for the Washington social scene. Today's discovery was a stunning blue evening dress which Bonnie plans to wear for the election evening gathering in their home.

"Yes, you won't believe what I found, the perfect garment for our election party. It's a blue dress and according to the sales lady, the only one of its kind in Washington. Sheila was green with envy!"

Preston and Bonnie's relationship has become very measured, very orchestrated, over the years of their marriage. Bonnie, being somewhat younger and much more gregarious than Preston, revels in the Washington D. C. social scene, and is constantly in motion preparing for parties, political gatherings, or promotional events for the newspaper. Preston, however, tolerates this only as a price to pay for a functioning marriage of a man in his level of society. Lately he has shown a marked lack of interest in these events, so all the impetus has been placed on Bonnie.

"That's wonderful, dear. Let's have one more drink before dinner."

For anyone qualified to closely monitor Preston Daley's manner, a diagnosis would quickly emerge; here is a man greatly troubled by someone, or something, and experiencing extreme conflict at the moment. This man with the iron fist in the office is slowly turning into jelly internally. His carefully crafted persona of strength is melting at an alarming rate. Whatever he is experiencing within himself must be horrendous, but Preston Daley is a master of never divulging his thoughts. This terribly tormented man is being eaten alive, but he continues to charge on with a fighting, stiff upper lip. Preston always fights. Preston always attacks. Offense is what has proven successful for him in life!

Bonnie, however, is just the opposite. In our nation's capitol, one never knows what is real. All of life, or all of political life, might be characterized as nothing but a plastic facade. Diplomacy permeates everyone and everything. Accepted ways of behavior and interaction must be followed at all times. Wanting to wring the neck of an acquaintance at a cocktail party must be held in check, with that ever present plastic smile, as one cordially discusses the current situation in Bosnia, or whatever, with him. Bonnie thrills in this environment. She loves the interaction with important and famous people. She can't get enough of it. This is her outlet. This makes up for a personal life with Preston which isn't very interesting or exciting; her life with him never has been, but it does provide a perch for her to fly off happily into the wonderful world that is Washington, D.C.

Maxwell announces, "Dinner will be served."

Mr. and Mrs. Daley begin the trek to the second floor Dining Room, taking the elevator which is located at the far end of the Great Room, near the Billiards Room. Arriving on the second floor, they exit the elevator and proceed left to the Dining Room, passing the stairway leading up to it from the Great Room. Two place settings at the end of a long dining table await them, carefully caressed by soft candle light from a single large silver candelabrum. Dinner will take exactly 45 minutes. At its conclusion, another Wednesday evening will pass into history.

Chapter Three

At 2 p.m. on Sunday afternoon a C'est Magnifque catering van can be seen parked in front of the town house immediately adjacent to the Daley residence. Two men slowly walk toward the rear of the van, beginning the process of unloading trays of hot and cold hors d'oeuvres to be taken inside. An expecting servant, Andre, greets his new arrivals with a warm "Bonjour," and then a slew of "des orders" on how to proceed with the work at hand. "Allonsy!, Fermez la porte!, Mettez-le sur la table!"

This is the town house of Count Pierre Le Blanc, a recent arrival to Georgetown. In no time this most witching and magical man has become the Georgetown dandy, the shining star of the Washington social scene, by charming all of society with his many graces . . . and especially so, the Georgetown ladies. His quick "fait la baise" to each "femme sensationnelle" in any room instantly disarms all and sets the stage for an evening of total "elegance." Count Le Blanc *is* the new sensation of Georgetown this season!

All that is known about the Count is that he is French, and is from an old French family that owns a winery located in the Chablis wine district of France. Such clouded mystery surrounding this most appealing man just increases his aura. Count Le Blanc is obviously a world traveler, for he is quite able to converse at once on any topic, be it travel, apparel, cuisine, wine, classical music, fine art, jewelry, or even politics. He is a most perfect addition to any gathering, and to the ladies, a welcomed fresh breath of air from most of the resident males.

Next door in the Daley townhouse, the mood is quite different; Preston Daley has been in a morose state since arising at 5 a.m. this morning. He's currently on the phone, conferring with a business associate about a major change contemplated for the Statesman.

"Why is he qualified?"

"What work experience does he have to indicate competence for this position?"

"Would you hire such a young individual for such an important position?"

Preston Daley is talking to his only friend in the world, art dealer Roscoe Blusher, about current conditions at the Statesman and this radical move contemplated for the newspaper.

"Do you think this has any chance of working?" There is a long pause . . . then . . .

"It Has To!"

"Dearest, you must begin to get ready for Count Le Blanc's party. It is after 2:30!"

Bonnie tries to coax Preston along, but to no avail. He is going nowhere at 3 p.m. this day! Today, Sunday, has become a working day for him.

"Darling, you go along. I'm busy working on something for the paper. I'll try to stop by later."

One more social disappointment for Bonnie!

Comfortably past 3 p.m. Maxwell escorts Bonnie next door to Count Le Blanc's townhouse, which is a beautifully preserved brick building belonging to a Danish diplomat who has recently been reassigned from Washington. The Count was quite fortunate in being able to find and rent it fully furnished at a moment's notice. Properties of this level are hard to find in Washington quickly.

Andre gaily greets both at the front door. "Bonjour Madame," and taking Mrs. Daley from Maxwell, escorts her inside to the gathering. From his position near the fire place, an ever observant Count Le Blanc quickly spies his new arrival. In a flash he greets, "Ah . . . Madame Daley; Oh, I so wish you were Mademoiselle!"

Mrs. Daley melts.

Count Le Blanc notices Mr. Daley is not present.

"Is Monsieur Daley not feeling well?"

"Thank you for asking. No, he is busy working on something for the newspaper. Preston will try to join us later."

"It is my gain he is not here!"

Mrs. Daley melts again.

Moments later Andre returns with a silver tray containing two crystal glasses of white wine.

"Madame, please try this."

Count Le Blanc secretly whispers in Madame Daley's ear; "This is Le Blanc Chablis Gran Cru, the finest wine our Chateau can offer, and the finest Chablis in the world! Please, enjoy it with me."

A totally impressed Madame Daley takes the glass of wine from Andre, holding it by its bowl.

"Madame, like this!"

Taking the other glass from Andre, by the stem, Count Le Blanc places the base of the wine glass between his index finger and thumb.

"We must never bruise the wine!"

Madame Daley appreciatively adjusts her position, likewise placing the base of the wine glass between her index finger and thumb. She radiates with confidence, for the Count has made a special effort to instruct her on one of the finer points of wine etiquette. The Count knows all! His guidance will be invaluable; she will be able to correctly appreciate this sample of the finest Chablis in the world.

"Now we are in a position to savor it properly. Take a sip; hold it on your tongue. Can you detect the scent of green apples . . . ahhhhhhh . . . and the slightest hint of lemon? Mmmmmmm . . . it's so perfectly balanced, with lively acidity, but not overwhelming at all. Note the flinty mineral aroma that distinguishes Chablis from all others."

Count Le Blanc tips his wineglass somewhat, allowing the wine to coat the upper reaches of the bowl. Then he holds his glass upright.

"Look, you can see it has legs!"

Madame Daley tips her glass, and then holds it upright.

"It has legs!"

"Madame, you have just experienced the finest Chablis in the world, not the lesser quality Chablis found in large jugs here in the States. All true Chablis is from the Chardonnay grape, but labeled Chablis because that's the area in France it's grown."

Senator and Mrs. Stratum presently arrive. The Count excuses himself to greet his new guests. Mrs. Daley moves about the room to socialize with the others.

"Madame Stratum, a most special welcome to the most beautiful lady in all of Washington; Oh, I so wish you were Mademoiselle!"

Madame Stratum melts.

Andre approaches with two more glasses of white wine.

"Madame, please try this."

Count Le Blanc secretly whispers in Madame Stratum's ear; "This is Le Blanc Chablis Gran Cru, the finest wine our Chateau can offer, and the finest Chablis in the world! Please, enjoy it with me."

"Madame, like this . . . ."

About the room, if one cared to notice, lady after lady is seen holding a wine glass between an index finger and a thumb. The phrase, *"We must never bruise the wine,"* followed by, *"It has legs,"* wafts thru out the room!

Next door, in the Daley townhouse, Preston Daley pours a scotch and soda and continues to work alone.

In Count Le Blanc's kitchen, Andre quickly unscrews another gallon jug of white wine.

Chapter Four

Hushed whispers permeate the newsroom at the Statesman. Who is this new addition, this skinny adolescent looking individual with pimples who appears as though he hasn't even begun to shave? What possible function could he have at the Statesman? It is Monday morning; the important meeting between Fasset and Mr. Daley is approaching.

"Fasset, Greatbanks, come into my office!"

Fasset and Greatbanks stand up and begin the walk toward Preston Daley's office. Basil Fasset looks at this newcomer in surprise, this kid now walking beside him who answers to the name of Greatbanks, and wonders what is happening, why is this newcomer being summoned to his meeting with Mr. Daley? Is he being replaced today by this kid? He hasn't been able to sleep for five consecutive nights, fretting about what to present to Mr. Daley this morning, and now he will be placed on display to this juvenile specimen of humanity who probably has never had a real job in his life! Can things become any worse for him?

Both participants seat themselves at Mr. Daley's work table, with Fasset feeling most apprehensive about what might soon take place. Preston Daley does not sit; he stands at the head of the table, ready for action. He appears ready to strike.

"Fasset, this is Ackerley Greatbanks, our new Information Technology manager. We have languished for too long a time around here without first rate technolgy.

Greatbanks is going to bring us up to speed for the 21st century. You will be working under his guidance.

Oh, Terrific, thinks Fasset! How humiliating. Things just got a lot worse!

The Statesman has never stepped out of the mid-20th century in its development. Preston Daley has made sure of that, always going with what has proven successful and profitable. He firmly believes, "Don't go looking for trouble and ruin a successfully running business venture!" The paper has not embraced any of the new technology available to enhance itself. It doesn't even have a web site!

"Greatbanks, explain to Fasset exactly what you plan to implement to jump-start our new push forward, to increase our readership!"

A squeaky voice pipes up.

"Ya know, the Statesman, is like so stuck in the last century. It's in a time warp. It's like a car parked at the side of the road. The 21st century just cruises right by. No one like reads printed newspapers anymore, ya know. Printed newspapers are like so old fashioned."

Fasset sighs, the paper is doomed! Where did Mr. Daley ever find this freak?

Preston Daley has not slept for five nights either. His paper is disintegrating right before him, on his watch. This push with Greatbanks is a last resort. He must do something for the Statesman, and he must do it at once! He must not allow the Statesman to sink any further. Greatbanks comes highly recommended, a cracker jack new age geek. He's his last hope!

Fasset looks toward Mr. Daley, totally unable to distinguish what his boss is thinking or even believing right now, but one thing he knows for sure, Preston Daley is betting everything he has on this kid!

Greatbanks continues. "Ya know, more books are sold in e-form now than hardcopy. That is like so cool. E-copy is so with it. The Statesman must join the 21st century with an e-edition, like right now!"

Preston Daley interjects, "Fasset, what have you come up with?"

Basil Fasset, at this moment, is feeling like a pair of black Patton leather shoes at a sock hop; "ya know, he is like so out of place!" How can he follow this first presentation, especially when Mr. Daley seems to be so enamored with his new geek?

"Mr. Daley, I have been thinking all week about the paper's direction. We aren't selling excitement any longer; we aren't providing something special for our readers to look forward to each week; we are not creating a reason for them to want to buy our product. Our editorial direction must change, and we must become a morning newspaper to be relevant in today's world. Until we do so, we will continue to flounder."

Fasset takes a deep breath.

"Mr. Daley, my first recommendation is to restore full coverage, to resume a complete presence on Capitol Hill. Second, we should restore special series reporting. Then we need to address sports coverage and . . . . ."

Greatbanks fondles an electronic gadget in front of him; it's about the size of a small notebook. He appears to be not the least bit interested in what Fasset has to say, as he slouches in his chair.

Mr. Daley, however, is very interested. Fasset has not told him one thing he wanted to hear. He interrupts Fasset.

"Fasset, what you are proposing will cost money, lots of money. We don't have it. We cannot go in that direction."

There is total silence in the room.

With this statement, Preston Daley has just announced to the world the defining problem at the Statesman. Ever increasing costs have squeezed profits! There is absolutely no developmental money available. Mr. Daley finds himself in a box. Over the years he has been forced to routinely approve reductions in quality as an off-set to increasing costs. Predictably, these reductions in quality have further reduced readership. The obvious result of each round has always been a new plunge in profits, and the end result of many years of such a strategy is Mr. Daley's current dilemma . . . *the Statesman is locked in a death spiral!* There is no way out of a death spiral. This is what has been so tormenting to Preston Daley lately!

The squeaky voice breaks the silence.

"Does anyone know what this is?"

Greatbanks holds the electronic gadget up for all to see.

"This is new. With it I can like download books, newspapers, or magazines like anytime I want, and ya know, carry them around with me like all day long. This is so with it, I can like read the Statesman any time of the day, ya know, anytime, anywhere!"

Mr. Daley's interest perks up visibly with this statement, and at what he is now viewing before him.

"You mean you can obtain all that on this little gadget? How many books, how many magazines, how many newspapers can it hold?"

"Ya know, Ya can't count that high!"

Mr. Daley can't quite believe his good fortune. What is being presented to him by Greatbanks at this precise moment is the magic bullet he's desperately been seeking to save the Statesman. Greatbanks has provided it on his very first day. What a concept! What a gadget! With it the Statesman will have a rebirth. It will join the 21st century and thrive again. For Mr. Daley, the matter is settled!

"We will initiate an electronic edition of the statesman, immediately. Can you have it ready by the first of the month, Greatbanks?"

"Sure, Ya know, maybe sooner!"

"That's what I like to hear. Well done, Greatbanks. Fasset, make sure Greatbanks has everything he needs to make this happen. Whatever he wants, you get it.

This is our top priority project. Make sure it is well publi-

cized up to D-Day and afterwards!"

Preston Daley now smiles for the first time in ages; he's beginning to anticipate the warm, caressing wind of positive change that will soon engulf the Statesman; he's beginning to feel the real sense of optimism that will surely accompany it. Once again there will be hope for his newspaper. The Statesman will survive and prosper in a new golden age of glory that will begin today! The great weight, on his shoulders for all these months, is about to be lifted . . . and it is about to be lifted by this newcomer called Greatbanks!

Chapter Five

One cannot begin to fathom what the hapless Fasset now feels, or the extreme humiliation he will soon experience at Greatbank's beck and call! This new arrangement is more than any valuable, long-term employee should ever have to endure. At this moment, the only thing keeping Fasset from walking right out the door is the promise of a full pension, waiting for him at normal retirement age, in less than six months. Somehow he must persevere.

Around the newsroom employees view the new human tornado called Greatbanks rapidly getting to work; Information Technology is his passion. He quickly organizes his work space, and requisitions whatever equipment he can find, anything currently available lying around idly in the office. There isn't much to tempt him. A mousey nasal command slices thru the newsroom!

"Fasset, I need a new computer with at least 2 GHz of CPU, 2 GB of RAM, and a 1000 GB Hard Drive, a laser printer, and an update of this software, immediately!"

Employees roll their eyes at the spectacle now taking place before them. Fasset jumps at this latest command. He has no idea what the letters, GHz, CPU, GB, and RAM, even stand for, but hustles to comply immediately.

"You'll have them by 1:15!"

From inside his office, Preston Daley observes the theatre taking place in the newsroom, with Fasset on the phone ordering computer equipment! Any employee, caring to look, might even detect an ever so faint smile on Mr.

Daley's face. Something is quite different in his demeanor, since his meeting with Fasset and Greatbanks earlier this morning.

Look at poor Fasset, the man with this huge increased burden now placed upon his shoulders! His life is quickly becoming a living hell! How can he juggle two jobs? The printed edition of the Statesman must still be delivered as usual, with all the hassle associated in that mission, plus he has just inherited this new distraction with Greatbanks. It is all too much to ask of any one man!

"Fasset, I'm going to need an assistant, someone to type input for me."

"Fasset, I'm going to need those PDF files."

"Fasset, does anyone around here know the first thing about HTML?"

Basil Fasset slams down his phone. He is in the middle of dealing with a major issue, a press breakdown caused by batch of faulty newsprint. Here could be a major disaster in the making for today's paper. The presses for the printed edition must start in just over one hour. He must find a way to resolve the issue at once, and all he has to work with are more rolls of the same defective paper. A solution must be found, and found quickly, or the afternoon home edition will not be on time! And then, there is Greatbanks!

Another mousey nasal command slices thru the newsroom.

"Fasset, I need a copy of the Statesman's logo."

Fasset pounds his desk in frustration. He gets up and walks directly to Mr. Daley's office.

"Mr. Daley, I can't do this. I can't work with this kid any longer. I am totally unable to do so!"

"Fasset, you can and you will! This is the number one priority around here. Do we understand each other on this?"

Fasset's head drops. He says nothing, turns around, and meekly walks back to his desk.

"Greatbanks, you'll have the logo in ten minutes."

Others in the newsroom say nothing. They know what they are seeing.

Fasset sits at his desk seething with anger. Never before has he felt such animosity toward his employer; right now he is boiling and he is stuck! Nothing can be done about it! He can only take more and more of whatever is dished out by Mr. Daley, and more and more of the same from this little twerp Greatbanks, until his retirement day. For 37 long years Fasset has endured this nightmare with Preston Daley, submitting to his tyrannical whims, but this is the breaking point. Greatbanks is Fasset's breaking point.

Fasset's devotion to the Statesman has cost him everything, his marriage and his life. Irregular, long hours spent at the paper contributed to his ruined marriage, and then eliminated any possibility of a social life from then on. He lost his house in his nasty divorce, and found himself stuck making alimony payments for years. But things became even worse for him. As he was pushed harder and harder at the Statesman by Mr. Daley, more and more alimony was extracted from his increasing paycheck by the court. Fasset was on an exclusive treadmill to nowhere, a treadmill which was only moving faster and faster day after day. Much like Mr. Daley, Fasset is a man with no real friends, and spends his very limited free time in his one-bedroom apartment watching old movies. This is the life of Basil Fasset, and the sum total of what he has to show for a lifetime in the newspaper business, and working for Mr. Daley! How can he find a way to hold on now? His retirement date can't arrive soon enough!

"Fasset, Any chance of getting that computer equipment before 1:15?"

Chapter Six

Lieutenant Jack Beebe sits hunched over his computer screen, squinting at a list of recently reported bunco cases. This veteran police investigator's nose is beginning to smell something very fishy in Georgetown. Lately he has been investigating a string of low profile, high pay-out burglaries involving expensive jewelry, but now . . . suddenly, there surface these new bunco cases. An inner something is telling him they may all be connected. It's just a hunch; they're completely different categories of crime, but Lieutenant Beebe senses a very sophisticated ring of criminals has moved into Georgetown and is taking over his jurisdiction.

The burglaries are of grave concern to him, because all of them targeted the social elite and were brilliantly executed with a laser-like precision, almost as if the thieves knew ahead of time where to strike. All break-ins were very clean, with no wasted effort; all were very professional with no trace of entry, and nothing left behind to aid investigators. The thieves just vanished, with almost a million dollars of fine jewelry, stolen since the first of the year. No traces of this missing jewelry have ever shown up locally, at pawn shops, or the underground sources used to fence stolen goods. These thieves are experienced, they don't make adolescent mistakes.

Lieutenant Beebe's office door opens. Sergeant Slaytor exclaims, "You may want to come down and witness this. An elderly lady is in the interrogation room right now, hysterically talking about her loss of $7,000 in a 'Pigeon Drop' scheme this afternoon."

Jack Beebe sighs; how do normal people keep falling for this old trick?

"I'll be right down."

This could be huge. It's the first time his officers will have the opportunity to talk to a bunco victim, literally within minutes of a crime. The lady may be able to shed light on the ring of thieves, or at least be able to provide some obscure clue or piece of information about them. Anything would help at this point. Lieutenant Beebe walks into the interrogation room, politely introducing himself to the woman.

"I'm Lieutenant Jack Beebe, and I want to do everything in my power to recover your money. Please, try to relax, try to settle down, and talk with me. You're in good hands. We are all professional law enforcement officers here."

The woman tries to compose herself.

The facts of the case are these. The woman is Edna Humphrey, a feisty 76 year old Georgetown grandmother. She was walking down Wisconsin Avenue returning from her bank when a very pleasant and honest-looking man approached her saying, "Pardon me, did you just drop this envelope?" She replied to him in the negative, so the man quickly opened the envelope to see what was inside. It contained a huge amount of money. The man exclaimed, "There must be $100,000 here. This is our lucky day. We can split it." Another man, overhearing the conversation, walked up to them and said, "I am an attorney. You cannot do that. It is against the law, but I know how to process this legally for you. Then it will be all yours, without question. I will do that for a 10% fee."

This seemed like the proper course of action to everyone. Ten thousand dollars were needed immediately to proceed. The attorney then made an offer; he would process it for free, for a 1/3 share of the money, but the nice man said that wasn't fair to Mrs. Humphrey. They would proceed with the original plan. However, there was a problem; the nice man had only $3,000. If Mrs. Humphrey would supply the other $7,000, she could keep $70,000 of the money, and he would be very happy with only $30,000. It was agreed.

The attorney took the envelope containing the money, and accompanied Mrs. Humphrey to her bank to make her withdrawal. By co-incidence his office was in the same building, on the 7th floor. She gave him her $7,000, and he said he would immediately go to his office to get started recording the serial numbers on the new-found bills. Mrs. Humphrey was to obtain the remaining $3,000 from the nice man on the street, who by then would have returned from his bank, and bring that $3,000 to the attorney's office at once. All paper work would take about a week.

When Mrs. Humphrey went outside looking for the nice man on the street, he hadn't yet returned from his bank. She waited for over 30 minutes, but he never returned. She then went to the attorney's office, which wasn't an attorney's office at all, but an employment agency. Hysterically she called the police.

"Mrs. Humphrey, try to remember everything that happened this afternoon, every little thing."

Have you ever seen this man before?"

"Does he look like someone you might already be acquainted with? How old is he?"

"Father Knows Best!"

. . . . "What?"

"Father Knows Best!"

. . . . "What?"

"'Father Knows Best' . . . you know, the TV show. That's the man!"

The detectives look at each other in puzzlement. What or who is "Father Knows Best?"

"The other man, the attorney, what did he look like?"

"Oh, he was nice too. I don't think he looked like anybody!"

"Mrs. Humphrey, try to recall clothing."

"The nice man was in a blue blazer, the other man in a dark business suit. Both were very handsome. I knew immediately they could be trusted. They had a civilized air about them. They were so honest and helpful."

The interview continues for about 1 hour. The detectives can tell it is beginning to wear on Mrs. Humphrey.

"Mrs. Humphrey, this is my card, Lieutenant Jack Beebe. I am personally going to follow this case. Tonight, tomorrow, the day after, I want you to keep a piece of paper and a pen handy. When you think of anything, anything at all about what happened today, immediately write it down. I can't tell you how important this is. The slightest detail may be the clue that breaks this case wide open and gets these predators off the streets. We will find these people for you. You have my word on that!"

One of the officers escorts Mrs. Humphrey toward the door of the interrogation room. As she approaches it, she pauses for a moment, then turns back to Lieutenant Beebe with a puzzled look on her face. After thinking for a several seconds, Mrs. Humphrey makes a statement.

. . . "Thorny!"

. . . . "What? . . . . Thorny? . . . . Thorny?"

"Yes, Thorny . . . Ozzie's next door neighbor . . . he's the other man!"

"Thorny! . . . . . . Thank you Mrs. Humphrey."

Jack Beebe returns to his office deep in thought. He now knows his suspects are not low life grifters, but two very presentable middle aged men. This fact confirms his suspicion; these men are professionals. They know what they are doing, and will not make sloppy mistakes.

The Lieutenant turns to his computer. Who is "Father Knows Best?" He must find out at once. A quick

"Google" produces a web page and a photo; here is his prime suspect! Yep, he has just found a photo he can work with. This man really does look quite honest. It is obvious why people fall for his smooth talk!

And who is Thorny? A second "Google" produces a match, TV show Ozzie and Harriet's next-door neighbor, Thorny. Lieutenant Beebe looks at this new photo; of course, another pleasant looking individual.

Thank you, Mrs. Humphrey!

Chapter Seven

"Fasset, when can I expect my assistant?"

Employees in the newsroom are so conditioned to the mousey sound now screeching above them, they don't even look up; they hear it countless times, each hour of each day. Whatever they may think of Greatbanks personally, professionally they can all see this kid works very hard! No idleness on his part, ever! He is totally event driven! Already Greatbanks has the Statesman web page up and running, and is closing in on the day when an e-edition of the Statesman can be released to the public. Employees are beginning to feel a certain excitement within their office. Even Mr. Daley is becoming more civil in his dealings with all his employees, something never experienced previously.

Poor Fasset looks tired and completely frazzled. On top of his already heavy work load, he has been assigned another responsibility, of composing the web page and editing what is presented on it daily. On this new web page, readers of the Statesman can view a portion of the paper, as a teaser, to entice them to subscribe to the full edition. Response so far has been very positive; Fasset's design concept displays his many years of training in the newspaper business, both in composition and in presentation. His 37-year career spent as a beat reporter, special series writer, news editor, and circulation manager are now showcased most positively in this new venture. Fasset is a true journalism professional.

"Fasset, come over here . . . right away . . . hurry,

hurry, hurry!"

With this outburst, a screeching Greatbanks seems to be signaling a kind of "Eureka" moment. Eyes in the newsroom turn toward their geek.

"Hurry, Fasset . . . hurry, hurry!"

The kid is really excited. This is not the kind of excitement associated with flight in danger; this is Christmas morning excitement. Something is up! Something is happening right now in the newsroom!

Mr. Daley comes to his office window to investigate the commotion. From inside his office, he has heard Greatbanks' exclamation, so now gazes out to witness what it is all about. Fasset quickly arrives at Greatbanks' work area. Greatbanks is jumping up and down, hardly able to contain himself.

"Slow down, Greatbanks . . . slow down. Everything will still be here 15 seconds from now!"

Fasset leans over Greatbanks' computer. He says nothing. He navigates the pages, one by one. Several minutes pass. The frown, that was so apparent on his face moments ago, disappears completely. A more relieved, relaxed, and composed face, at peace with the world, emerges. Fasset stands up with his arms folded across his chest, but says nothing. Greatbanks is still excitedly jumping up and down. All eyes are on Fasset. He looks down at the computer screen one more time, then, he looks directly at Greatbanks.

"You've done it! You've done it, Greatbanks. Nice work, Greatbanks!"

Fasset offers his right hand to Greatbanks; Greatbanks returns a cold linguini hand to Fasset. In the Statesman newsroom, employees see a representative from two different generations shaking hands, on equal footing, for the very first time. All employees know what has just happened. They stand, smile, and applaud. The excitement that has been building for several weeks is confirmed.

Mr. Daley emerges from his office door, and in a tone so unexpected, says, "Greatbanks, Fasset, *please* come into my office!"

This hastily called meeting is most cordial.

"Greatbanks, will you be ready with the e-edition by the first?"

"Sure, like whenever Fasset is ready with content!"

"Fasset, what do you need to do to finish your end? Have you planned promotion of the e-edition? Is the financial reporting system in place? Are you able to guarantee a non-interrupted flow of information to the e-edition? Are all these systems in place?

"Mr. Daley, we have 9 days until the first. I will be ready in 7 days. That leaves 2 days to 'tweak' the system for any malfunction. It's a tight schedule, but based on what I just observed, it is doable with a high degree of confidence. Yes, we'll be ready by the 1st!"

"Wonderful! That's great. Fasset, begin a full-blown promotional blitz right now . . . in the printed edition of the Statesman, on our web page, on the radio . . . get together with our public relations firm for assistance . . . use whatever means necessary to blanket the area with this great news and our opening date . . . we cannot afford one slip-up, not one!"

"Yes sir, Mr. Daley!"

Fasset and Greatbanks return to their work areas with noticeable smiles on their faces. The other employees in the newsroom feel a sense of relief also.

"Brenda, call Foster and Foster . . . set up a meeting for 4 p.m. this afternoon. No excuses from them, none. This is top priority. They *will* be here!"

Look across the room at Greatbanks. He is right back at work, without even taking a celebratory handshake or a celebratory break, trying to improve on what he has just constructed. He never quits!

What, the Statesman has a new employee? Its lovable

geek, Ackerley Greatbanks, is now being referred to as the "Ack-Man." The "Ack-Man" just "eats and chews up" news stories, faster and faster as he goes! This designation is a sure sign Greatbanks is finally being accepted by fellow workers. He has *worked* his way into their hearts.

Chapter Eight

Blusher's Art Gallery is located on Wisconsin Avenue, in the middle of Georgetown's commercial district. It's a well known first floor boutique on this main thoroughfare, and over the years has attracted a most discriminating clientele, both domestic and international in origin. Around Washington, huge sums of money are spent by the affluent, to obtain the "most perfect" specimen of fine art needed in completing a decorating project, especially if the project is in any way associated with the diplomatic corps, where no eye for cost is likely to be found. Proprietor, Roscoe Blusher, is a master of facilitation, the ability to aid in completion of any project, being able to supply just the right piece, at just the right price. The piece supplied always fits perfectly, and is usually the only one of its kind in Washington! It is this business model that has made Blusher's a very successful and profitable art gallery for many years. Roscoe Blusher is Preston Daley's best and only friend.

This afternoon Mr. Blusher is not to be found in his private office, located at the rear of the shop, but at his work station in the gallery proper. He comfortably sits behind a stunning Louis XVI leather-topped desk, totally engrossed in a recent issue of the international art trade publication, "Chroma." Walls all around him are adorned with beautyful original paintings: oils, acrylics, and some water colors. In a separate alcove near the center of the gallery, very expensive and most desirable pieces are tenderly displayed. "Giclees," reproductions on canvas, are to be found near the rear of the gallery and priced attractively for the more moderate appetite. Blusher's has something for just about anyone.

"Jingle, jingle, jingle," a tiny bell sounds as the front door to the gallery opens. In walks Preston Daley.

"Roscoe, wake up!"

Roscoe looks up from his magazine.

"Preston, how are you? No, I'm not sleeping; I'm totally consumed by this article."

He holds up the magazine for Preston to see.

"Recently, some very clever forgeries of paintings have appeared in southern France and Monaco. Experts have been fooled completely by the quality of the work. This is beginning to turn into an international spectacle, because some of the pieces were sold into the worldwide art market thru reputable dealers. One example recently showed up as far away as Tokyo. The perpetrators of these forgeries are a very talented lot."

"You haven't sold me any of those, have you?"

"Oh, no, it's been so long since you bought anything, anything at all! Only current serious collectors need worry!"

This good natured banter is only possible among the very best of friends.

"You've got me there, Roscoe, but things are about to change. Pour two cups of coffee, and I'll bring you up to date."

Blusher's Art Gallery has a professional espresso machine able to make the very best brew possible, one cup at a time, so while Roscoe busies himself grinding coffee, Preston walks through the gallery, browsing the current offerings. He notices the high quality of some of the works, called "giclee," located in the rear of the shop.

"Roscoe, these just get better and better."

"Yes, the technology is improving constantly. The new professional high quality ink-jet color printers can easily take a digital photo from a computer, and print it onto the canvas, to achieve an almost original look-alike piece. From a distance it's hard to distinguish between the two. Some artists enhance the print further with highlighting brush marks. It's a great way for them to expand the market for their works!"

Preston Daley pulls up a chair to Roscoe's desk, to receive his freshly-brewed cup of espresso.

"Oh, this is so good, only the finest at Blusher's!"

"Now, Preston, tell me what's been happening at the Statesman. The last time we talked, you were going to hire an Information Technology Manager."

"Yes, and I did. What a find! This kid has completely invigorated the whole paper. He works non-stop, and has developed an e-edition that will debut on the 1st. Just think, we will be able to increase our circulation with this new e-edition, with literally no increase in production expense. Most everything is already in place, so the new advertising and subscription revenue will fall right to the bottom line. I couldn't be more excited!"

"We must celebrate, Preston, with an artistic piece to commemorate this milestone?"

"Unfortunately, I don't have time for that now. I can only spend a few more moments with you today. So much is in motion at the paper, I cannot tarry, I must return to the office quickly."

Preston Daley walks toward the door.

"Jingle, jingle, jingle," it opens.

"Preston, I will find just the right piece for you to commemorate this momentous occasion!"

"Jingle, jingle, jingle," the door closes.

Alone, Roscoe Blusher returns to the task of reading

about international art forgeries. Some fifteen minutes pass.

"Jingle, jingle, jingle," Blusher's shop door opens once again. A very handsome, well-dressed man enters the gallery.

"Bonjour, Monsieur, I have passed by many times, but have never had the pleasure of entering, until today. I see some very familiar friends here, works of art that are dear to my heart. You have a talented eye for 20th Century pieces. May I have the pleasure of walking about?"

"Of course, would you desire a cup of coffee?"

"Merci Beaucoup, that is so very kind of you."

The impeccably dressed gentleman, in a blue blazer with an expensive diamond-adorned crest on his breast pocket, strolls thru the gallery, spending most of his time in the alcove area. Here he moves about in a regimented, regulated way, from painting to painting, as if formally studying each in some way, with no emotion what-so-ever shown by his enjoyment of the art. Then he moves to the rear, where the "giclees" are found.

"These are quite good. What a wonderful way for a person of lesser means to enjoy fine art! Do you sell many of them?"

"Yes, we do. They are very popular. Is there an item you would like that is not shown? I can obtain it for you; works from current artists are readily available."

"Thank you, no. My passion is early 20th Century Art. Unfortunately time is so pressing this afternoon, but when I am able to do so properly, I shall return and we can spend some time exploring 'cubism' together. I am Monsieur Le Blanc, Monsieur Pierre Le Blanc. Until the time, when we are able to meet once again, I leave you with a fond 'au revoir.'"

"Jingle, jingle, jingle," Monsieur Pierre Le Blanc exits Blusher's Art Gallery.

Chapter Nine

Excitement! What excitement at the statesman! Two days remain until the 1st of the month!

Fasset is at work early this morning, absorbed with his task of initial testing of the Statesman's e-edition. So far, so good! Fasset and Greatbanks, working together now, are a complete team, in perfect harmony with each other. Their electronic communications fly back and forth, from work station to work station; page after page of today's paper display upon their screens. Each checks line by line for accuracy, and then checks again; no errors are allowed, not one!

Mr. Daley can be found in his office, at his work table, making a feeble attempt at using his new electronic gadget. So far he hasn't found a way to display or read anything. He drops it on his table in disgust.

What really is of interest to Preston Daley this morning is the pile of papers stacked immediately to his left. Here are fresh reports of advertising revenue; the numbers are not at all good. The persistent decreases in daily Statesman circulation have produced huge advertising revenue shortfalls as well, and the continuing cash drain once again confirms to Mr. Daley the grave situation of slow bleeding taking place at the Statesman. But Preston Daley is not at all depressed this morning, even after glancing at these numbers, for he is confident he can change the paper's direction, and soon. When the new e-edition is activated, financial conditions should begin to improve rapidly. Mr. Daley is only interested today in the web page, and its advertising revenue. This data will give him some idea of what to expect when the e-edition becomes active.

CPM (cost per thousand impressions) is a new term to Mr. Daley. Greatbanks alerted him to it, and pointed out that these numbers must be watched closely. They will indicate the revenue from advertising that the Statesman will receive for every 1,000 page views served. In just a week, the numbers have doubled three times. That is robust growth, just what Mr. Daley had hoped for!

Out in the newsroom, intense developmental work continues to progress at a frantic pace.

"Fasset, check the City Desk. I need copy to finish this."

"Greatbanks, I'll compose the page and fire it right down to you."

All morning long, the two familiar voices exchange requests in staccato-like fashion.

"Crop that Capitol photo with the barricades, then cut the copy, and justify it."

"I need some filler for page 9!"

"Here's the dummy for the sports page."

"Rewrite page 23 and proof it."

"How did the font on page 47 get scrambled?"

"The gutter on the op-ed page is in need of a fix."

And finally. . .

"OK, let's put this baby to bed!"

The e-edition of the Statesman is finished. Greatbanks proudly projects today's printed edition on his computer screen; Fasset rushes over to share in the excitement. Both are viewing the e-edition for the first time, just as it will be viewed by the public when going "live" in two days. A final test tomorrow will be the last and confirming hurdle to cross.

Fasset has no further time to waste. A huge promotional effort for the e-edition was orchestrated by Foster and Foster, beginning a week ago. Fasset's part of that promotion was the printed edition of the Statesman and the web page. He must stay on top of it. All week long, short filler pieces have been added to announce the great event occurring on the 1st, with each piece emphasizing a different wrinkle of what will be available in the e-edition and how to take advantage of it. To Fasset's credit, he realized early that non-techie computer readers must be brought along slowly, and guided by hand each step in navigating the new e-world. If these "old world" readers won't embrace the "new," it is not likely the Statesman's circulation will increase by much. This was a brilliant marketing ploy on Fasset's part.

"Greatbanks, be sure the Banner in Bold Face is inserted for tomorrow!"

Fasset's quick check of a radio spot confirms Foster and Foster have covered that thread. *"Statesman Becomes Statesmen!"* is the ad's catchy slogan, emphasizing a metamorphosis, as *Statesmen* breathlessly move like ants all over Washington, announcing the great news. Clever! Some of the voices even sound like well-known current politicians. Around Washington, ads appear on the back of community buses and taxi cabs. Everywhere one looks in the Capitol, in any direction, some form of announcement is in place. Spots have even been taken in rival news publications. Foster and Foster have blanketed all of Washington with the great news!

On D-1, the last hurdle is passed. Final testing of the e-edition is completed without a hitch. All is in place for tomorrow, D Day.

****

D-DAY arrives! At 4:00 a.m. on the 1st, the e-edition of the Statesman becomes active for the very first time. Readers can begin to instantly download today's Statesman electronically onto their computers or hand-held devices.

The Statesman has joined the 21ˢᵗ Century!

Mr. Daley enters his office earlier than usual today. Greatbanks is already working.

"Greatbanks, what numbers are you showing? How many readers are identified so far?"

"Mr. Daley, it's like so early, ya know. I am seeing like about 1,000 right now, but it like increases right in front of me as we talk."

"Keep me informed each hour thru out the morning. Are there any problems?"

"Smooth like silk right now!"

"Good, Greatbanks. Stay on top of this!"

Mr. Daley walks into his office. The phone rings. It is Roscoe Blusher.

"Preston, I see it!"

"Roscoe, do you see the e-edition?"

"Yes, that's why I'm calling. I have it up on my computer right now. What an improvement! I can read the Statesman with my coffee at home now, and continue it anytime I wish, later at work. I love this new option."

Fasset arrives in the newsroom and is immediately noticed by Mr. Daley.

"Fasset, come to my office!"

Fasset doesn't even sit down; he goes directly to Mr. Daley.

"Yes, Mr. Daley?"

"We're 'live,' Fasset. Greatbanks says the number is over 1,000 already. We can't let this momentum die . . . keep up the promotional efforts for at least another 90 days . . . keep total focus on the e-edition . . . stay in touch with Foster and Foster . . . make sure they understand the importance of this . . . make sure they reinforce what has just been accomplished. Reinforce, Reinforce, Reinforce! Maybe make a new push, talking to the 'man in the street.' Reinforce! Keep this *hot*!"

"I'll do just that, Mr. Daley!"

Chapter Ten

Up and down the street in front of Mr. Daley's townhouse, all is dark and quiet. At this late hour, the street is totally deserted. The only illumination seen anywhere slyly peeks from behind a curtained third-story bedroom window of Count Le Blanc's townhouse, an illumination of yellow, glowing so mysteriously, forebodingly, that it might easily announce to any passer-by, "Come on in, watch something quite extraordinary and exciting taking place in here!"

Inside this closed door third floor bedroom, two individuals, Pierre Le Blanc and Andre, focus upon a computer screen and the chore before them. They are intently at work in this unfurnished bedroom, or artist's studio, with easels, semi-finished canvases, and the strong organic smells associated with paints and inks all about them.

Against one wall sits a sophisticated commercial ink-jet color printer, as well as a more common laser printer. Computer and camera equipment are strewn all over two work tables.

"Gaylord, hold it right there. OK, let's see what that does."

Gaylord? What is this? Something is amiss in this third-floor bedroom! Count Le Blanc has just addressed Andre as, Gaylord? The darkest of dark secrets is now out. Andre is not Andre at all, but one Gaylord Moreau, a frustrated starving artist by training, and a very successful art forger by occupation.

The computer screen flickers, then the laser printer begins to produce an image on paper. Gaylord retrieves it, critically examining the result.

"We're getting closer, Francois, we're getting closer."

Francois? What, another surprise? Yes, we discover now that Count Le Blanc is really the jet-setter, Francois Chevalier, a French playboy with a less than successful record of citizenship in numerous European cities. A most checkered past has he!

This evening, Gaylord and Francois are busy trying to produce a "giclee" print on canvas. The countless unsuccessful dry runs already attempted, hang as semi-finished evidence of this difficult goal. Whenever the acceptable finished product is finally achieved, Gaylord, the talented artist, will carefully paint over, creating a perfect forgery.

"Francois, there is still too much red. The picker is showing numbers of R=210, G=140, B=140. It needs more yellow. Reduce R to 160, B to 130 and then see what happens."

"Do you think it is the canvas? Is it white enough? Should we apply more coating?"

"No, Francois, it is a perfectly acceptable canvas as is. This last color adjustment should do it."

Francois and Gaylord are experimenting using a 6-color professional ink-jet printer with Piezo heads and sophisticated software, including Raster Image Processing (RIP) which takes over the printer's driver for a better job of color management and printing. Native resolution, digital photo image of the painting, is 200 ppi, to insure clarity. Interpolation is kept to a minimum. Canvas is archival acid free and water resistant. These two rascals obviously have some knowledge and expertise in what they are now attempting, in secretly birthing an artistic masterpiece in this third-floor bedroom.

Camera equipment found about the tables is varied. The two vagabonds have a most perfect selection of equipment to take digital photos of anything, anywhere, anytime under any condition imaginable.

One appealing and ingenious piece of equipment stands out from the others. It appears to be a piece of jewelry, in the form of a coat-of-arms or family crest, with cut-glass diamonds thru out. A very careful examination will uncover a camera lens surrounded by the diamonds. A rubber bulb, attached to a long cord, activates the camera to snap the photo. What a perfect piece of sleuthing hardware!

"Ready, Francois? Make a final soft proof."

"OK, here it is . . . looks good. I think we're ready."

The computer screen flickers, the ink-jet printer against the wall activates, and slowly a finished "giclee," of an original painting begins to emerge. Both can instantly see this is it, this is the result they have so painfully been trying to create. They have their "giclee." Gaylord carefully hangs it upon an easel.

"Tomorrow I will begin the painting. Let's make a couple more now for insurance."

At 3:10 a.m. in the early morning hours, the glowing light from the third floor bedroom extinguishes. The mischief is over for tonight. All is dark and quiet once more in the street below.

Chapter Eleven

Mr. Daley nervously stares at the file in front of him, knowing he must open it, this very first report of e-edition revenue. Two shaking hands tear open the folder.

Wow! The CPM numbers are huge! And look, for the first time in memory, revenue at the Statesman increased last month. The e-edition is a rousing success! Almost 10,000 new subscribers joined the existing readership of the Statesman, and this is only the beginning. Maybe another 10,000 next month, or even 20,000; then, more increases the following month! Readership will continually grow and grow as more and more will follow. It won't be long before total circulation will be back to 125,000, then to 150,000, possibly even to 200,000. What a profit bonanza that should be! The sky is the limit from here. Preston Daley knows he is about to make his mark, accomplishing what his father did before him, *growing the statesman!*

Preston grabs the phone and dials quickly, "bep, bep, bap, bep, bup, bop, bep."

"Roscoe, it is time to think about a commemorative piece. The first numbers from the e-edition are just in. Find me something worthy. We'll discuss this further Saturday night at the Club." Mr. Daley then walks to the doorway of his office.

"Fasset, come to my office."

"Yes, Mr. Daley?"

"Great work with Foster and Foster! Ten thousand new e-subscribers last month! Now, let's follow

through! Conduct a poll! Find out the new readership demographics . . . ages . . . incomes . . . interests . . . why they have joined our readership. Find out everything you can about them. Do it quickly! We must not allow them to slip away. Then make sure all are rewarded somehow, by supplying what was uncovered in the poll. Make announcements in both the print and e-editions about what will be forthcoming, so they have something to look forward to. Don't let them slip away! Don't let them slip away!"

"Yes sir, Mr. Daley."

Fasset returns to his desk with a mission. He first arranges a meeting with Foster and Foster.

"Brenda, please call Alex Foster! Have him here at 4 p.m. We have a ton of items that need attention immediately, today. No excuses, it is imperative that we meet at 4 p.m. today."

All during the day, whenever Mr. Daley looks out in the newsroom, he sees a parade of important Statesman employees huddled with Fasset. These are the departmental heads, the people who make things happen. Fasset is quickly taking the steps necessary to insure Mr. Daley's wishes become a reality.

In his office, Preston Daley sits for most of the day behind his desk, and just dreams about circulation numbers. This is his favorite thought today. Nothing at the Statesman is pressing, so he finds himself lazily doodling numbers on a pad of paper. As he writes, breath-taking figures instantly pop up to greet him. A Statesman circulation increase to 125,000 papers per day projects an increase in profit of $1,000,000 per year. At the 150,000 papers per day plateau, profit increases by $2,000,000, and then a whopping $5,000,000 of increased profit per year jumps out at him at the 200,000 papers per day level!

Preston can hardly contain himself. The good times are about to return! He thinks again about what Roscoe Blusher said to him, "I will find just the right piece for you to commemorate this momentous occasion!" Yes, this Saturday night will be the perfect time to gaily discuss this topic which is so dear to his heart, and something missing from it for far too long . . . an art purchase!

****

Every Saturday evening, Preston and Bonnie Daley have dinner at the Town Club, a very exclusive Georgetown gathering spot for over 100 years. Maxwell has the limousine waiting for them at the front door at precisely 7:00 p.m.; Mr. and Mrs. Daley then arrive at the club at 7:15; they sit down for cocktails at 7:30, on the very same couch, at the very same time, each and every Saturday evening, listening to background tones of pleasant piano music muffled by conversation. On most Saturdays, Roscoe and Honey Blusher are their dinner companions.

The Town Club "reeks" of money. Look at the huge Gainesboro painting gracing the wall above the couch where the Daley's are presently enjoying cocktails, and over head is a breath-taking crystal chandelier which softly illuminates the entire area. Hurried waitresses walk about presenting drink after drink to well-dressed members and their wives. This *is* the "upper crust" of Washington, the Washington political and social elite, relaxing and entertaining as they do each and every week-end.

Roscoe and Honey Blusher are immediately spotted by Bonnie as they enter the room.

"Honey, that dress is stunning. Did you find it at Gala's?

Bonnie knows the answer, having already picked over it this past Wednesday on her outing with Sheila Stratum.

"Yes I did. I fell in love with it at once, but there were so many new things to choose from."

Mr. and Mrs. Blusher sit down on chairs perpendicular

to the couch, and proceed to order drinks. Some minutes later, with polite small talk completed, Preston motions to Roscoe that he wishes to speak with him in private. He moves to the chair next to Roscoe; Honey now sits on the couch next to Bonnie to continue talking about clothing at Gala's.

"Roscoe, this has been some month at the Statesman. Our e-edition totals 10,000 already, and is growing rapidly. I am quite impressed with the results of our move into the e-world. This is something we should have embraced long ago. We still have much ground to make up."

"Yes, I've been reading the Statesman at home before going to the gallery. It is my quiet time each day. Isn't modern technology amazing, allowing me to do all this with such ease? This e-edition is only going to grow and grow."

Roscoe, slyly, doesn't mention anything about art work, but Preston, by now bubbling with anticipation and excitement, is dying to bring up the subject. He can stand it no longer.

"Roscoe, I've got to have something to commemorate this event. What ideas do you have?"

"Slow down, Preston, these things always take time; the piece selected must be absolutely perfect. I've been thinking . . . I currently have . . . one possibility . . . that might be the perfect candidate. . . . We will need something contemporary . . . from an established artist . . . which captures all of the excitement of recent events at the Statesman. It must be bold, yet have staying power . . . just like the e-edition. And it must be a desirable piece, which will only grow and grow in value in future years . . . much like your Virtuoso Saludo. That was an excellent purchase, by the way. The piece I have in mind . . . *"Illusions"* . . . is a Claude Gravois. Here is a well-placed contemporary artist, in the Photo-Realism style, who, in my opinion, will only become more and more desirable over the years. This piece is expensive . . . of course . . . but among friends we certainly can work out something in price. . .

Chapter Twelve

It is Election Day evening; inside the Daley townhouse, a festive looking great room waits for invited guests.

All is in readiness. The natural beauty of the room is enhanced on this election evening, as each painting in Mr. Daley's art collection reflects a tender light shining down upon it from above. On the long wall, an impressive new acquisition, *"Illusions"* by Claude Gravois, is lovingly displayed beside the most valuable piece in the collection, the Virtuoso Saludo. Two giant crystal chandeliers sprinkle the room with muted rays of light. One can almost feel a soft glow of gold tones and strategic shadows, which create an invisible veil all around.

Maxwell has a bar placed at the foyer, to greet guests as they arrive, and to encourage the social contact which is to follow. A party at the Daley townhouse is always an event to be remembered!

Bonnie Daley, in her sparkling new blue evening dress, hurriedly walks about the Great Room, in making final checks of preparations. Maxwell enters the room, accompanied by Andre, who has been loaned for this occasion by Count Le Blanc, and both begin to set up the bar. It is almost 8 p.m.

"Maxwell, be sure the alarm is turned off. We don't want any unsolicited police visits!"

"I'll take care of it, Mrs. Daley."

Maxwell mentions to Andre that the silent alarm will sound 40 seconds after the front door is opened, so he excuses himself for a moment to disarm it.

"Preston, darling, you're finally home; our guests will begin arriving any moment now!"

Preston Daley has just arrived, somewhat later than usual, after spending the day observing the political landscape from his office vantage point. Some early returns in key states have already been announced, but many more are due in just a few minutes at 8 p.m.

"Dear, give me ten minutes to change. I will hurry."

Into the Great Room walk four musicians, members of a Dixieland band, who will provide exciting tunes all evening long. All are dressed in black slacks, white shirts with red stripes, red suspenders, and white flat-brimmed hats reminiscent of the early 1900's. They begin to set up near the billiards room, but during the evening plan to walk about the house playing in various other rooms. Dixieland music just invigorates and lifts a party to a higher plane.

Shortly after 8 p.m. the first guests begin arriving. Maxwell and Andre immediately offer liquid refreshment from the bar at the foyer, while Bonnie walks over to greet each, and to make sure each guest feels welcome.

"My dearest Joan, what a divine dress you are wearing this evening, is it from Gala's?"

By 8:45 p.m. the Great Room pulsates with guests. Dixieland music echoes from the Library. Look! Standing in front of Mr. Daley's new art acquisition is a group of ladies, and each is holding the base of a wine glass between their index finger and thumb; all are gathered around one very handsome-looking gentleman wearing a blue blazer. He's Count Le Blanc!

"Count Le Blanc, you must tell us all about your chateau and winery in France."

"Count Le Blanc, is Chablis really Chardonnay?"

"Count Le Blanc, that gleaming diamond crest on your blazer pocket, what does it represent?"

"Ladies . . . ladies . . . ladies . . . . How can I answer you all? Time is so short . . . it does not permit a proper discussion of our chateau, but yes, Chablis is really Chardonnay . . . and this is my family's crest, some 500 years old now."

Maxwell approaches with a silver tray containing two crystal glasses of wine. Bonnie Daley moves closer to whisper into the Count's ear.

"This is Le Blanc Chablis Gran Cru, please enjoy it with me."

Maxwell could only find this lone example in all of Washington, and at $300 per bottle, probably just as well, but Bonnie had to have it this evening to present to Count Le Blanc.

"Merci Beaucoup! What a treat this is, from the most beautiful hostess in Washington!"

Count Le Blanc slowly takes a sip.

"Ahhhh . . . the green apples . . . the lemon . . . the flinty mineral aroma . . . you are far too kind, Madame Daley. You make me feel so welcome this evening; I feel as though I'm at home, once again, in France. I can't thank you enough . . . Oh, I so wish you were Mademoiselle!"

Mrs. Daley melts and radiates as she sips her wine. To her unsophisticated pallet, something seems a little bit different about it this evening. This wine is so wonderful . . . so much more complex and so much smoother than she remembers . . . and as she tips the glass, the legs are more robust.

"It gives me great pleasure to remind you of your homeland, Count Le Blanc."

"Count Le Blanc, we're planning to travel to Monte Carlo . . . I suppose you've been there many times?"

"Of course, Madame Stratum, many times; there is nothing quite like Monte Carlo in the entire world. I love to visit . . . the grandeur . . . the elegance . . . the old world charm of a by-gone day . . . when will you be traveling?"

"In early January, before Congress re-convenes. Do you

have a favorite hotel and casino?"

"All are quite exquisite, but my personal favorite is the Casino de Monte-Carlo. I love stepping back into time, an elegant time over 100 years ago, while playing there. Do you plan to stay at the Hotel de Paris? You must eat in the Louis XV restaurant. Oh, I'm becoming so excited just talking about it!"

Great smiles are on the faces of all the ladies. Monte-Carlo sounds like such a magical place!

"Ladies, I've been noticing, your eyes have been focused upon this painting. Do you like it?"

"Oh, yes, we do," is the common response, in unison. "It looks so real. How can an artist paint something that looks like a photograph but is really a painting?"

"That is the magic of a paint brush in the hands of a talented artist. Look at the reflective shadows cast by the chrome and glass . . . and the stances of the people walking by . . . perfectly portrayed by the artist. What is his name, Gravois . . . Claude Gravois?"

Bonnie Daley chimes in. "Preston has just purchased this painting to commemorate the launching of the e-edition. Roscoe Blusher told us it represents a style called Photo-Realism, where everything is in sharp focus, with subject matter of common, everyday scenes, not the staged compositions of classical paintings. I especially like it; it reminds me of the sidewalk view to Gala's Department Store!"

The other ladies instantly shake their heads in agreement.

"Yes, yes, of course it does. We can see it now!"

Count Le Blanc shifts his view to the Virtuoso Saludo painting displayed next to it.

"This painting is so interesting to me. I believe it is from one of the Fauves, a Post-Impression artistic movement. Look at the wild brush strokes and strong, pure colors . . . the simplification . . . the abstraction . . . it just makes one want to walk into the painting.   This artist, Saludo . . . what a master!"

These interesting comments, and a detailed knowledge of so many topics, are what make Count Le Blanc so welcome in social gatherings, but this evening the ladies aren't at all interested in, or excited by, the Saludo; they comment that they by far prefer the Gravois.

Bonnie Daley now turns to acknowledge, and greet, a new gentleman to the group.

"Please, join us, Basil; Count Le Blanc, I would like you to meet Basil Fasset . . . ."

Chapter Thirteen

Basil Fasset's anticipation mounts . . . a package has just been delivered to his desk, a package from Foster and Foster that he has anxiously been expecting all month long. Here will be the results of the new poll of e-edition subscribers.

Basil opens it quickly. Hmmmmm . . . age . . . income . . . education . . . all very similar to existing subscribers. Likes . . . dislikes . . . all are very similar. Reason mentioned for subscribing to the e-edition . . . more flexibility . . . and the ability to read a morning paper . . . and then his jaw drops!

The next data can't be correct . . . these new subscribers aren't new subscribers at all; they are existing Statesman readers who have embraced the morning e-edition and have switched! Very few new subscribers are represented here, statistically. Basil just stares in disbelief at the report in front of him; he is frozen in fear. This can't be correct, this just can't be correct! And what can be done about it now? Nothing! It won't be long before Mr. Daley becomes aware of this; better begin preparing, and bracing for the fall-out that will quickly come. It won't be pretty. Mr. Daley has bet everything he has on the e-edition, and this report indicates he has absolutely nothing to show for it! Mr. Daley won't take it well. Oh, retirement can't come soon enough!

"Fasset, get into my office, now!"

Oh, here it comes!

"Yes, Mr. Daley?"

"Fasset, how do you explain this?"

Preston Daley throws a handful of papers at Fasset's feet. Statesmen employees see the developing inferno quickly intensifying in their employer's office; they see the familiar body language, and instantly look the other away. Nothing need be said. Everyone knows. The "old" Mr. Daley is back!

Fasset gathers the papers from the floor. He scans the numbers. He can see the drop in print edition revenue. He can see the increase in e-edition revenue.

"Fasset, Greatbanks has grown our subscriber base! Just look here! Ten thousand new subscribers last month! He's the only one working successfully around here. You have done nothing at all, nothing at all for the Statesman; in fact, you have continued to allow the print edition to stagnate even more this past month. Fasset, with you in charge, this trend of printed circulation losses just never, never ends! We dropped another 8,000 subscribers last month. This is the end, Fasset. I am replacing you immediately as circulation manager. From this moment forward, Greatbanks will become the new circulation manager. You will work under Greatbanks until your retirement next month, or you can leave today! It is up to you. That is all!

After several moments of silence, Fasset says nothing, turns, and shuffles back toward his desk with his head down and in a state of complete despair. He shakes his head thinking . . . is this the thanks I get for 37 years of effort? Mr. Daley has no idea what is happening. He continues to believe the e-edition is prospering and will save the Statesman. He hasn't a clue that it is just stealing existing print readers; last month's revenue increase was a one-time only event in which the same subscribers were counted twice. This month, as the new e-edition readers dropped from the printed edition rolls, the real truth surfaced in the fresh numbers. It was also confirmed by Foster and Foster's poll. I'll let Greatbanks break the news to him.

Fasset knows what he now must do. He slowly begins the process of packing his belongings. His career in journalism is over. He speaks to no one. All his contemporaries do not need to be told what has just occurred in Mr. Daley's office. All are currently witnessing a career of thirty seven long years in the newspaper business ending badly today for Fasset, right now before them, on this, his last day of employment at the Statesman.

Fellow workers can view Greatbanks in Mr. Daley's office, receiving his first round instructions. The body language shows the "old" Mr. Daley has returned in full force. One can only imagine what is going thru Greatbanks' mind as he stands in place for the very first time, taking what is dished out by Mr. Daley. The Statesman is totally his watch now. For Ackerley Greatbanks, there will be nowhere to hide from this point on, nowhere at all!

The far door to the newsroom quietly opens, and then slowly begins to close. Not a sound is uttered by anyone. A transparent Fasset disappears for the last time behind this door, and into a harsh world which beckons him from beyond.

Chapter Fourteen

Jimmy Talley parks his newspaper delivery truck at the far corner of the parking lot, by the glazed donut shoppe, then hops out and quickly rushes toward the front door in a mad scramble to claim his weekly reward.

It is Saturday evening, 9 p.m., and Jimmy is making his customary early delivery run of the advertising and magazine sections of tomorrow's Sunday newspaper. This little treat is all he will have to look forward to, before his grueling six-hour run depositing Sunday newspapers all around town.

"Hi Jimmy. A dozen of the usual?"

"Yea, Sal, and fill my Thermos with lots of hot, black, coffee!"

Jimmy will immediately eat two of the glazed donuts with some coffee, and then parcel out the remainder over the next six hours. It will get him through the night.

"Hey Jimmy, who are you picking for tomorrow, Cowboys or Redskins?"

Two patrons in the shop motion to Jimmy to come over and sit with them.

"Redskins don't have a chance. Dallas is the best team! Nobody can stop Dallas, not even the Packers!"

Conversation in the shop turns to pro-football and potential NFL pairings. Two other patrons loudly express their differing opinions, and a great football debate begins with nobody at all noticing that the Statesman delivery truck is no longer in the parking lot. To any onlooker outside, the truck's two red tail lights become smaller and smaller as it cruises farther and farther away from the donut shop in Georgetown traffic.

****

In the street outside the Daley townhouse, all is quiet and dark. A large truck is approaching . . . look, it's a Statesman delivery truck! The driver quietly parks immediately in front of the townhouse door, and two shadowy figures emerge, one carrying a covered parcel. Both easily gain entrance to the Daley townhouse. One ... two ... three ... four ... five ... they are in the foyer. Six ... seven ... eight ... the figures separate, nothing said, moving in different directions in the Great Room. Nine ... Ten . . . Eleven . . . one figure moves an occasional chair from the wall. He climbs on it. Fifteen ... sixteen ... seventeen ... the other figure is near the Virtuoso Saludo painting. Thirty one ... thirty two ... thirty three ... their work now completed, the shadowy figures retrace their steps, walking back thru the foyer. Thirty seven ... thirty eight ... thirty nine ... they are outside. Forty . . . the truck pulls away quietly.

****

Ding ... ding ... ding ... ding ... ding ... ding ... ding ... ding ... ding ... a fire alarm rings at Central Station.
"OK men, come on, let's get it moving!"
Within 30 seconds, firemen are ready, dressed for action, and climbing aboard the pumper. Its screaming siren signals to traffic to clear the way; a moving fire truck pulls from the fire house into the street, loaded with all the excitement associated in the motion of a fire run.

****

At Horizon Security, signals of a break-in at the Daley town house are recorded. Protocol dictates an automatic police call after no sounds are detected within the residence. More sirens are now heard in Georgetown.

****

Inside the Town Club, a most festive dinner is in progress, with a well-dressed waiter preparing Steak Diane tableside to great acclaim by the Daleys and Blushers. Preston Daley and Roscoe Blusher are preparing to dine. Preston Daley's cell phone begins to vibrate.

"Yes. Yes. When? Yes, I'll be right there."

The others at the table stare at Mr. Daley in amazement, wondering what could be happening this evening, what could be so important?

"A fire at our house, and also a break-in . . . we must return at once!"

"Preston, how terrible! We must go with you."

Preston Daley calls Maxwell immediately from his cell phone.

"Maxwell, we will meet the limousine at the door in two minutes. There is a fire and break-in at our house . . . just moments ago. We must return home at once.

Hurriedly, the dining party rises from a table of unfinished meals, walking rapidly from the dining room. Looks of astonishment from other diners greet them as they proceed toward the door. Maxwell already has the limousine waiting; all enter, and their anxious ride home begins.

Maxwell wastes no time, quickly swinging the limousine into traffic, and recklessly begins the process of driving thru Georgetown traffic, trying to shorten the fifteen minute trip to five minutes. He runs every yellow or red light encountered, and passes all other vehicles in his way. In just over six minutes the limousine enters the Daley neighborhood, but Maxwell finds their street is roped off.

Two fire trucks and several police cars are scattered about in front of the Daley townhouse, all with lights flashing. Most of the front porch lights of immediate neighboring townhouses are illuminated. Count Le Blanc, standing in a bath robe at his open front door, talks to anyone who will listen.

"This is quite an evening of neighborhood excitement! No, I didn't hear or see anything at all, not until the first fire truck arrived."

Count Le Blanc looks down the street and sees the Daleys hurriedly rushing toward their townhouse.

"Madame . . . Monsieur . . . what has happened?"

"Count Le Blanc, we don't know. We just received a message of a fire and a robbery and returned home as soon as we could." Bonnie breathlessly speaks to the Count.

Count Le Blanc and the disrupted dinner party stand on the Count's front steps, gazing at the front door of the Daley townhouse, which is wide open at this moment with a stream of firemen constantly entering and exiting. Most of the lights on each of the four floors are illuminated, but no sign of a fire is visible, and not one fire hose is inside the premises. A distinguished looking fireman approaches the Daleys.

"Mr. Daley, Mr. Preston Daley? I'm Captain Stoker. We are just finishing. We have secured the building, and no traces of fire have been detected at all, anywhere within the structure. I can't say positively at this time, but I would guess that somewhere, a malfunction of the fire alarm system caused all of this."

"We can't have that. I pay a large stipend each month for protection. This will not be allowed to stand. Tomorrow I will have Horizon Security out here first thing, the very first thing."

Mr. Daley appears irritated and furious as he speaks!

Lieutenant Jack Beebe approaches Mr. Daley.

"Mr. Daley, I'm Lieutenant Jack Beebe. Concurrently

with the fire alarm, we received a break-in alarm. I must ask you to walk thru your dwelling with me to ascertain if anything is missing. I'm sure you can appreciate this, knowing there have been other burglaries in Georgetown recently."

"Of course, by all means, let's do so immediately!"

Preston Daley is very anxious to check the safety of his art collection. He follows Lieutenant Beebe into the townhouse. They stand in the Great Room. What a beautiful sight! Not one painting is missing! Not one! Nothing in his art collection is disturbed! A smiling Preston Daley relays this information to a doubting Lieutenant Beebe, whose critical glance has just noticed what appears to be a footprint indentation on an occasional chair. Lieutenant Beebe says nothing.

Mr. Daley then begins the walk-thru of his townhouse house with the Lieutenant. Nothing detected out of order . . . or missing . . . Mrs. Daley's jewelry is safe . . . her wardrobe is secure! All is well. This evening has turned into a giant false alarm and an exercise in precaution. Horizon Security will certainly hear about this tomorrow!

Mrs. Daley, the Blushers, and Count Le Blanc stand at the bottom of the spiral stairway, waiting for Mr. Daley and Lieutenant Beebe to return from the second floor to the Great Room.

"All is well, dear. The Lieutenant and I have just verified it."

Bonnie appears so relieved, exclaims, and immediately motions to Maxwell, "Let's try to make a positive moment from this terrible situation tonight. Our guests will want to celebrate with us . . . a libation . . . and something to eat. See what we can procure in a moment's notice, Maxwell."

As the sound of fire trucks exit the neighborhood, talk in the Daley library has already turned to safety and precaution . . . then Preston Daley's cell phone vibrates.

"What, Greatbanks . . . our truck is missing? Find it!"

Chapter Fifteen

The next morning, Sunday morning, 9:15 a.m., a Horizon Security truck arrives at the Daley townhouse. Two workmen gather tool boxes and a ladder from the back of the truck, then make their way to the front door; the door opens before they have a chance to ring the bell. Preston Daley, less than cordial and in a bellicose manner, steps outside into the morning sunshine, to instruct them.

"This disaster from last night must be accounted for. I don't care what it takes, do whatever is necessary to find the problem, and resolve this situation at once, so this never, ever, happens again. Are we in agreement on this?"

"Yes sir, Mr. Daley. We will find the problem."

Mr. Daley returns inside the townhouse; the two workers begin the process of setting up their equipment at the front door. The elder worker exclaims to his partner, "He's a little testy this morning, must have been some circus around here last night. Can you believe it, a fire alarm and burglary alarm, all at the same time? Can't recall that ever happening before!"

The younger of the two workmen climbs the ladder and traces along the upper regions of the door-jam for any signs of forced entry. The other does the same for the lower regions; he then toggles the door lock mechanism several times in an effort to determine its effectiveness.

"This all seems to be in order."

Pulling a cell phone from his pocket, he makes a call. Beep ... boop ... beep ... bap ... bap ... beep ... boop.

"OK, we're ready for a test. We will now close and open the front door."

One ... two ... three ... seventeen ... eighteen ... nineteen ... thirty eight ... thirty nine ... forty seconds pass. An alarm sounds in the central office. This information is relayed back to the workers.

"Great, this door works perfectly."

One by one, all other outside doors and windows are checked and verified by the two workers. No problem can be found anywhere. They then turn their attention to the smoke detectors. Each detector, in each room, is independently checked and verified. All easily pass inspection; all work perfectly. One, in the Great Room, appears somewhat dirty, so is cleaned as a matter of course.

"Well, the only remaining item to check is the control box. Since all the remote elements are functional, our problem has to be there," mumbles the older worker. "Get a new unit from the truck, Bob."

Shortly the worker removes the old box, and quickly hot-wires a new unit to the home's electrical system. After four hours of work, the senior workman is ready to face Mr. Daley with his verdict. He summons the home owner.

"Mr. Daley, we have checked all components of your system. All are in perfect working order. I can only conclude that something, perhaps a power surge, corrupted your control box. We have replaced that unit. The battery back-up is perfectly operational. You are in good shape now. Your system is in perfect working order."

"This must never, never happen again. Never! I expect perfection when it comes to security and safety! From now on, we will schedule a complete system check once per year. Schedule that for next year right now!"

A still agitated Preston Daley, who at least seems to be somewhat satisfied with the worker's explanation, scratches his signature on the work order, and sends the two workmen off to their next stop.

Chapter Sixteen

Lieutenant Jack Beebe can't get the image of the man standing next to Mrs. Daley from his mind. What was it about the man . . . the man standing in a bath robe in the Daley Great Room . . . on the evening of the false alarms . . . which keeps returning to his consciousness? The man appeared so smooth, so likable, so trusting; the kind of person you think you've known all your life . . . yet on Saturday night Lieutenant Beebe had no idea who he even was. Something was familiar about him, but what? Why does he keep thinking about the man now, why does the man keep reappearing, over and over, in his mind?

The Lieutenant sits at his desk this Monday morning, browsing the weekend log. Some strange events from the past weekend have grabbed his attention. Of course there was the double alarm at the Daley townhouse, but there was another . . . a stolen newspaper delivery truck. It was recovered less than one hour later, with nothing missing and everything in good order. The official report stated probable cause as possible "teenage prank." OK, I'll buy that, it's possible, he thinks, but if so, it's the second of two seemingly innocent cases in one evening? That's a stretch. I hate coincidences!

Nothing is going right in the Lieutenant's world right now. Chief Loss is pressing him; the Chief is tired of excuses, he wants arrests! The jewelry robberies have not been solved . . . every trail has gone cold . . . progress in the bunco cases has come to a standstill with no arrests . . . a conclusion of any of the cases pending cannot be expected any time soon. Lieutenant Beebe is beginning to feel the pressure. These thieves have him baffled completely; they are very, very good . . . real pros.

He also feels badly for Mrs. Humphrey. The Lieutenant hasn't been able to produce anything that could lead to the recovery of her money or the arrest of the culprit. He promised her he would do that. Every lead has been a dead end so far.

Lieutenant Beebe decides to open the folder on her case once again; he jots down what pertinent facts are known into a time line. At the end of the time line he places the photo of Father Knows Best. Look! How strange! Well, at least one puzzle is solved today. The man in the robe in the Daley Great Room looks similar to Father Knows Best! That's why I've been thinking of him lately. Silly!

Lieutenant Beebe's consciousness drifts back to the two unexplainable events of the last weekend. He thinks to himself, connect the dots . . . connect the dots! Isn't that what top flight investigators do? Pulling out a sheet of paper, he makes two columns, the first column . . . stolen truck, the other . . . false alarms. He writes down the pertinent known facts.

Event	Stolen Truck	False Alarms
Time (p.m.)	9:10	9:24
Place	Geo'town	Geo'town
Category	robbery	false alarm

On the surface, no commonality shown at all, but . . . . . wait . . . isn't Mr. Daley the owner of the Statesman? That was a Statesman truck that was stolen, wasn't it?

Commonality	Mr. Daley	Mr. Daley
Commonality	Statesman	Statesman

This is a new angle to work on. Was Mr. Daley the target, or was the Statesman the target? But the target of what . . . there was no crime. Let's follow this further. The footprint on the occasional chair in the Daley Great Room . . . really looked suspicious to me Saturday night, but nothing was reported missing. No crime at all. This is really troubling. It doesn't seem likely that a footprint would be allowed to remain on a chair for long, especially not in that room. It's really hard to believe. What's going on here? Am I so desperate to solve a crime that I'm trying to produce one? I'm making no progress at all on the other cases, but wasting time chasing moon beams here, thinking about a crime that wasn't a crime? No! No! I hate coincidences. I hate coincidences! Follow all leads; every small detail is important!

Call Mr. Daley now, have him check the house again. Maybe he missed something in all the excitement Saturday night. Also, the security system, did Mr. Daley have his security system evaluated since then? I must know every detail. Call him now to investigate.

Just seconds later on the phone . . . "Mr. Daley, this is Lieutenant Beebe. Pardon me for interrupting you this morning; I am following our investigation of the problem on Saturday night. Could you help me . . . has anything turned up missing since Saturday . . . could you recheck everything thru out your house again this evening . . . has your security system been evaluated since then? . . . Yes, yes . . . yes, and what was discovered? . . . May I have your permission to talk with Horizon Security? Thank you for your assistance, Mr. Daley."

I will need to talk with the men who made the service call to the Daley home. Horizon Security isn't far from here. I'll arrange a meeting when the men return from their last call this afternoon.

Shortly after 5 p.m. Lieutenant Beebe arrives at Horizon Security, and begins talking to Bill Shock, the manager.

"Mr. Shock, we are investigating the double false alarm Saturday evening at the home of Preston Daley."

"Oh yes, that was a strange event. Apparently a control box malfunctioned for some reason. We replaced it and the system is in perfect working order now."

"I know, I talked with Preston Daley this morning. I would like to speak with the workmen who made that service call. Have they returned yet?"

"As a matter of fact they have; that is their van just pulling into the lot."

Mr. Shock signals to the men, "Vern . . . Bob, come over here for a moment!"

As the men approach, Lieutenant Beebe introduces himself, and begins the process of explaining his investigation.

"It would be very helpful if you could relay to me the results of your investigation of the security system at Preston Daley's house. Please, tell me everything you found, every little detail, and what corrective action was taken."

Mr. Shock interrupts by offering to produce the inspection report; he walks into his office to retrieve it while the Inspector continues to interview the workmen. The older worker, Vern, becomes the main spokesman.

"We found no evidence of any break-in, either in the doors or windows. Each door, and each window, was checked individually, and verified with the communications center here. We then did the same for the smoke detectors. All checked out positively with the communications center. The only remaining option was to replace the control box, which we did."

"Think back, did you notice anything suspicious anywhere?"

"No, we saw nothing suspicious at all at the site, but later, after replacing the control box, and upon examining it back here, the box appeared to be perfectly functional. Strange!"

Mr. Shock returns with a copy of the inspection report,

handing it to Lieutenant Beebe.

"Here, Lieutenant, this is for you to keep in your investigation."

"Thank you very much, Mr. Shock."

Lieutenant Beebe's ringing cell phone redirects his focus.

"Yes, yes Chief! I'll return at once.

"Thanks again, men. I've just been called back to headquarters!"

Lieutenant Beebe turns and walks toward his car, to return to his office and Chief Loss. On his drive back, he thinks over and over . . . something is here, I just know it . . . I just know it! Revisit all the facts . . . revisit all the facts. I hate coincidences!

Chapter Seventeen

Lieutenant Beebe's short drive back to the police station takes only seven minutes. Chief Loss is waiting impatiently for him, pacing back and forth as the Lieutenant walks into his office. Instantly Lieutenant Beebe can sense this will not be a pleasant meeting.

Chief Loss strikes immediately!

"What have you discovered . . . what have you found . . . what new evidence do you have on the burglaries? Tell me you have something, Jack . . . anything; the mayor and city council are putting unbelievable pressure on me for some results. These are very powerful people who were robbed, and they are not, and will not, stand still for this. Our jobs are all on the line here, whether you want to believe it or not!"

"Chief, it's just a hunch, but I think the double false alarm Saturday night has something to do with all of them. I think the thieves tried to strike again, but something went wrong. They were foiled in their attempt. The answer is in the Daley townhouse somewhere, I'm sure of it."

"Lieutenant, how do I tell the mayor that my lead investigator thinks the answer to all these unsolved crimes lies in a place, the home of an outstanding community citizen, and a man I am well acquainted with, where no crime at all has even taken place? I'll be laughed right out of his office. You've got to do better than that, Jack. Go back to the facts of each of the burglaries; there must be a common thread somewhere. *Find it!*"

Jack Beebe walks from the Chief's office toward his own. How many more times must he look at the evidence of these crimes? Somewhere, there has to be something. As the Chief said, find it!

Sergeant Slaytor, who is leaving for the day, passes him in the hallway and casually mentions, "We received an un-solicited tip this afternoon about the double false alarm Saturday evening . . . an elderly lady called and mentioned that she saw a Statesman delivery truck on her street just before the first fire truck arrived. She said she thought that seemed rather strange, at that time of the evening. I put the information on your desk."

"A Statesman truck on the Daley's street at 9:00 p.m.?

"Yes, that's what the lady said."

"Thanks Slaytor, I'll get right on it."

Back in his office, Lieutenant Beebe sifts thru a pile of messages until he comes to the message from the lady in question. Here it is . . . yes, just as Slaytor said; this could be critical. If it checks out, it places both cases together. We'll have a smoking gun. We'll have commonality. She must be called at once.

Lieutenant Beebe places the call; an elderly sounding lady answers the phone.

"Mrs. Stead, this is Lieutenant Beebe from the crime investigations unit . . . yes, I'm calling about your comment to our office earlier today . . .

"Lieutenant Beebe, I want it understood from the begin-ning, I am no admirer of Preston Daley, and no friend of his, but I want to help out the police if I can. I'm very con-cerned about the rash of crimes in Georgetown lately; in fact, as an elderly lady I'm overly concerned about them. That is why I watch my surroundings constantly; you can't be too careful in this time."

"Yes, this is so true, Mrs. Stead. Tell me about what you saw, tell me about the Statesman truck. How did you happen to notice it?"

"Well, at that time of night, there is not much traffic on our street, especially large delivery trucks, so, of course, I would certainly have noticed it. On the side panel, and printed in large letters was, *The Statesman, One of America's Great Newspapers,*" so there was certainly no question. Normally I probably would not have thought anything about it, since Mr. Daley lives right down the street, but then the fire truck arrived, and I thought, that's strange! The more I thought about it, the more it bothered me, so that's why I decided to call you today. Lieutenant, don't think that I am an old lady with nothing to do, and just over reacting on some minor observation to gain attention. You can never be too careful these days."

"No, not at all, Mrs. Stead, we are grateful for your observation. Every single piece of evidence builds on the others, and on the sum total, so we can never know in advance what will sometimes tilt a case in our favor. Every piece of evidence is important. You can rest assured that our conversation will remain confidential. Thank you again, Mrs. Stead, for your call and your observation." The Lieutenant hangs up.

Well, there it is. We can place a stolen truck at the scene of no crime! I can't go to the Chief with that!

Lieutenant Beebe opens the investigation folders and looks at the time line of the two cases again. Yes, the truck was reported missing before the fire alarm and the attempted burglary were sounded, but Mrs. Stead is an elderly lady. What if her time recollection was off, by just a little bit? What if the truck had a valid reason for being on Mr. Daley's street and was there just before it was reported stolen? That is a possibility that must be checked out. Lieutenant Beebe calls the Statesman.

"Hello, may I speak with Basil Fasset, please?"

"I'm sorry, Basil Fasset is no longer employed at the Statesman. Would you like to speak with Ackerley Greatbanks?"

". . . . . Ohhhhhhh . . . yes, please."

Lieutenant Beebe thinks as he waits for Ackerley Greatbanks . . . Basil Fasset, gone? He's been at the Statesman just about forever . . . I don't recall hearing he retired.

"Is this Ackerley Greatbanks? You must be the new Circulation Manager? Tell me, how long has it been since Basil Fasset left the Statesman?"

A short conversation ensues with Ackerley Greatbanks bringing Lieutenant Beebe up to date on the time frame surrounding Basil Fasset's departure, but Greatbanks volunteers he cannot comment further on the specifics of the case.

Lieutenant Beebe exclaims, "I can't believe this, I didn't even hear from him before he left, this was all so sudden. Anyway, I am investigating the stolen delivery truck from Saturday evening. What can you tell me about it?"

"Well, it just like dropped off the face of the earth for one hour, ya know, then was recovered in a strip-mall parking lot. Like *Wow*, nothing was disturbed, and our driver was able to complete his run, like nothing happened, ya know."

Lieutenant Beebe remains silent for several seconds. "Tell me, Ackerley, it is Ackerley, isn't it . . . was there any reason for that truck to be on Mr. Daley's street that evening? Is that part of the route?"

"I don't believe so, ya know, but I must check with Jimmy Talley, the driver. He is like not due back until 11:00 a.m. tomorrow morning. I'll ask him and like report back to you then."

Lieutenant finishes the conversation, then thinks . . . What is going on at the Statesman. Fasset was a professional, this kid Greatbanks sounds so juvenile. I will need to talk to Fasset sometime soon and sort thru this. I hope this is not another coincidence? I hate coincidences!

Chapter Eighteen

Rita softly comments to Mrs. Daley, "Are you all alone today, Sweetie?" This manager of Gala's Lingerie Department speaks discreetly to Mrs. Daley, not wishing to broadcast any personal information thru out the store.

"Yes I am, Rita; Mrs. Stratum is in Monte Carlo, and my husband is in New York City for a gathering of newspaper publishers, so here I am, all alone today. I just hate this time of year!"

"Spend as much time here as you wish, Sweetie; we have a number of spectacular new items that were just placed out this morning. I know you will find something that is perfect for you."

Rita turns and walks back behind the counter while Mrs. Daley continues to peruse the new lingerie items in a half-hearted manner. Her heart is not into anything today.

From far across the room, a man watches the developing scene carefully. He slowly walks toward Mrs. Daley, in a most stealthy way, saying nothing . . . he is just behind her now . . . she has no idea he is near . . . she continues to sort thru the lingerie offerings. Then Mrs. Daley turns . . . *"Oh . . . Count Le Blanc!* You startled me; I didn't know you were even here."

"Ah, Madame Daley, the most beautiful lady in all of Washington, may I call you Mademoiselle this morning? I see you are all alone; may I assist you in finding something very special . . . a very special something for only you?"

With these comments, Mrs. Daley's spirit takes a 180

degree turn into positive territory. The Count has a way of doing this to her, or any woman in Georgetown for that matter, and on this depressing January morning, what a pleasant, uplifting development!

"Count Le Blanc, I was just admiring these." Bonnie holds up a couple of items. "What do you think?"

"They are gorgeous . . . Oh no, Mademoiselle, over here!"

The Count gestures toward a manikin modeling a daring, scanty two piece red garment covered with a see-thru veil of black, most certainly meant for only the most beautiful of aspiring young starlets.

Softly he whispers to her, "This is for you. I would die to be the one to see you model it. Do you like it, Mademoiselle? May I purchase this piece for you?"

Now, what can Mrs. Daley say? The count has just made her an offer she can't refuse. Of course, she must have it! She's in a great mood now. Bonnie knows her body is still fine, perhaps not as fine or as young as it once was, but at 48 years of age she easily looks 15 years younger, and will be able to carry off this piece perfectly.

"Oh, thank you Count Le Blanc. I would love to model it for you," whispers Bonnie, in a low, throaty, coquettish tone.

In a flash the Count presents the item to a more than a little impressed Rita for wrapping, then concludes his purchase by exclaiming to Mrs. Daley, "We must now relax in the 9th floor restaurant, and enjoy what remains of our day. Such a beautiful lady should never be left alone in a large city such as this."

Rita's eye brows rise.

In the 9th Floor restaurant, Bonnie Daley and Count Le Blanc are guided to a 2-top table, conveniently placed far away from the main traffic pattern of the restaurant, and begin to enjoy the skyline of our nation's capitol. The dome of the Capitol Building is their most prominent architectural feature.

"We must order a special bottle of wine for you, Mademoiselle, as an aperitif. May I select something? Shall we keep it light, something to enjoy before our meal, perhaps a white wine from California?"

The Count begins the process of studying the restaurant's wine list. It's a much more complete list than he would have expected from a department store restaurant . . .

"Ah, here is something interesting, let's try a California Sauvignon Blanc . . . these wines have racy acidity and fresh floral notes to them, a perfect complement to Mademoiselle's fresh floral and racy side!"

"Oh, Count Le Blanc, you are just awful . . . I love it!"

Bonnie Daley is feeling on top of the world at the moment. This day did start badly, but now she is exhilarated, on a cloud, and having lunch at Gala's with the most charming man in all of Washington. She thinks . . . Sheila won't believe this, Sheila will have nothing on me; I will be able to hear all about Monte Carlo from the Count right here in the restaurant, without ever leaving the country. The table conversation quickly turns to a discussion of Monte Carlo.

A second glass of wine has almost been consumed when the waitress returns to the by now effervescing couple, to take lunch orders. "Are we ready to order? Would you like another bottle of wine?"

The Count jumps right in, "By all means, another bottle! It was exquisite! Bonnie, do you have a suggestion for lunch, perhaps a house specialty to go with the wine?"

Bonnie blushes somewhat, knowing she's on the spot, because all she's heard about the pairing of wine with food is "white with white, red with red."

"Count, I love the lobster pot pie here, it *is* a house specialty."

"Perfect, two lobster pot pies it will be, and salads on the side!"

Their waitress nods, jots down the orders, and comments, "This is an excellent choice." She then excuses herself to obtain the second bottle of wine.

"Mademoiselle, I am so happy I have run into you today, you have brightened everything for me."

Bonnie sits up a little straighter in her chair, her mood elevated yet another notch by that comment.

"Mademoiselle, Tell me . . . why are you here, all alone today?"

"Well, every Wednesday Sheila Stratum and I come to Gala's for the day, but she is in Monte Carlo this week. Preston is in New York City for a couple of days attending a gathering of publishers, so here I am all alone . . . until you arrived to rescue me."

"I love the sound of that, a damsel in distress rescued by her Count!"

Bonnie melts.

"I see the Statesman has a new circulation manager. Did Monsieur Fasset retire?"

"Well, I guess he did, but Preston never talks about events in the office with me. It was all so sudden, I think something happened."

Their waitress approaches with the lobster pot pies on a silver tray, readying for serving by placing them upon a folding serving stand, tableside.

"Mademoiselle, you were so correct."

The Count looks at the two pot pies, and then slowly turns to gaze at Bonnie, softly saying . . . these two look marvelous . . . May I pour you another glass of wine?"

Bonnie blushes . . . yet again.

Oh, what a spectacular luncheon it is! Bonnie is beginning to feel more and more like a Countess. It may be the wine, or it may be the atmosphere in the restaurant, or it may be the Count himself . . . whatever it is, Bonnie Daley feels absolutely royal and giddy at this moment. The meal is quickly consumed, with only one final glass of wine remaining in the second bottle. The Count carefully divides it between the two of them, stating, "Mademoiselle, I am so totally happy. Your presence has made my day complete. Your beautiful blue eyes have changed a grey January morning into a beautiful summer afternoon in France. I so wish our short time together today will never end."

"Count, it is so early, it doesn't have to."

"Oh Mademoiselle, I am so happy to hear you say that; make me the happiest man in the entire world . . . will you do something very special for me, will you model . . . will you model the lingerie for me . . . . . this afternoon?"

. . . . "Oh yes, Count . . . yes . . . I will."

****

Bonnie and the Count enter the elevator, on their way to Room 1147 in the Arcanum Hotel, which is directly across the street from Gala's Department Store. Bonnie cheerfully thinks . . . Oh, that rascal, the Count! He had this all planned before hand! How impressive! Her head is still spinning from the events of the morning and the wine at lunch, and she relishes the fact that the Count would go to such an effort to carefully plan and write this little theatre that she is now acting out. How can she not be totally impressed? He has read her thoughts completely, like some old familiar book . . . this is what she wanted all along. Being with the Count is like being on center stage, only the center stage of the world!

"We are here, Room 1147." "Click," the plastic pass key unlocks the door. "Mademoiselle, welcome to my chateau."

The door opens; Bonnie looks in. Oh, is she impressed! The Count has obtained an entire suite of rooms; they are so elegantly and beautifully furnished. To greet her as they enter are a vase of flowers and a silver container, which is packed with ice and a cold bottle of Champaign. The curtains are drawn, with the low pleasant glow of many soft lights reflecting around the room.

"My Count doesn't ever miss a step! You've had this scene prepared and waiting this entire morning . . . just waiting for me to arrive."

"For my Damsel in distress!" . . . the Count holds up the bottle of Champagne . . . "while I uncork this, perhaps Mademoiselle would like to slip into something completely new . . . and something far more comfortable . . ."

A bubbling Bonnie quickly disappears behind a closed door off the sitting room. Count Le Blanc begins the process of uncorking the Champagne. It seems that only seconds elapse. Now the far door of the room tentatively opens . . . a bare leg to the knee dangles from behind it . . . then a peek-a-boo head leans forward, with the mischievous smile of a calculating vixen. Bonnie emerges from behind, only now she is a fiery-red candy cane covered with a see thru black veil wrapper, and saunters . . . slowly, toward the Count. The two meet; they embrace for the first time. Bonnie's two-piece lingerie slips to the floor, piece by piece; the Count's bath robe falls on top of it . . .

"Ohhh . . . Count Le Blanc" . . . the uncorked bottle of Champagne goes unnoticed . . .

END PART ONE

PART TWO

Chapter Nineteen

Dark clouds and icy conditions permeate the newsroom at the Statesman this January Monday morning. Yes, it is mid-winter. Yes, Preston Daley has returned from New York City. The mood here is absolutely arctic. What caused all this? Whatever could have happened to Mr. Daley in the Big Apple? Whatever could have happened to the Big Man, or, did something else happen, and not in the Big Apple?

Employees can see Greatbanks standing still, receiving yet another round of Mr. Daley's wrath. It is the third time this morning. Greatbanks just stares at the floor now as Mr. Daley pummels him with another long-winded tirade composed of verbal lashings and whippings. Employees can hear nothing, but they can all see Mr. Daley's gestures; body language tells the entire story. Greatbanks, as was Fasset before him, is now a beaten man.

Employees are being treated to the fall-out from Foster and Foster's report; Mr. Daley is livid! Greatbanks has had the rather unfortunate task of presenting the news to him this morning; the fall-out, as Fasset had predicted, is Titanic. Mr. Daley had bet everything on the e-edition. He was so optimistic at first, but now it is clear to him that the e-edition is not going to save the Statesman, as he had so hoped it would. The good feelings of the past couple of months are turning out to be short lived, and only a mirage obscuring a longer-term death spiral; the era of good feelings is officially over at the Statesman.

"Greatbanks, I don't want to hear any excuses, not one! I expect you to move forward, to increase circulation. That is what must happen immediately. You were brought in here to do just that. Adjust, be creative, make things happen. I don't want any more excuses. I want results. I demand them. Produce them, and at once!"

Greatbanks knows he is in way over his head in this job. It's not his fault; things just happened too fast to him. Mr. Daley was so impressed with his work on the e-edition, so mesmerized by his new technology, that he believed Greatbanks and his technology were the answers to everything. Mr. Daley thought Greatbanks was the magic bullet, all that would be necessary to produce results; somehow conditions would magically change with Greatbanks in charge. Well, it didn't pan out that way for Mr. Daley. It wasn't even close.

Greatbanks most certainly needs help right now; he needs lots of help . . . and he needs it today. He must do the unthinkable; he must contact . . . Fasset . . . at once! Quickly Greatbanks searches for a number scribbled down on a piece of paper in his wallet. He dials it.

"I'm like going to need to talk to you immediately, in 15 minutes. Can you meet me somewhere? OK, 15 minutes at your place."

Greatbanks hangs up, and walks from his office toward the door; he exits the news room.

****

Basil Fasset's one room apartment is only a short distance away, Apartment 226 in the Vacuous Arms Apartment complex. Greatbanks' heart pounds as he approaches the door, not knowing what awaits him on the other side, but knowing he must have this meeting with Fasset in any event. He reaches for the door bell; it chimes, and two seconds later an unshaven, rather relaxed looking Basil Fasset opens the door.

"I knew I would be receiving this call eventually. How bad is it?"

"Very bad! I'm ready to quit."

"Greatbanks, come in and let's talk this over."

Fasset ushers Greatbanks into his poorly furnished, untidy, and most depressing looking dwelling. Greatbanks can see dirty dishes everywhere, in the sink and all along the kitchen counter; some clothing is strewn on the floor, toward the bedroom.

"Let me fix you a cup of coffee. It will only take a minute."

Fasset walks to the sink, grabs two dirty cups, quickly rinses them out, then opens a jar of instant coffee and heats some water in the microwave. Greatbanks sits down; he can see that Fasset is in the process of writing something on his computer, which is open on the dining room table.

"Like what have you been doing with yourself in retirement? Anything exciting?"

"Just trying to keep myself occupied. I'm doing a little writing, and consulting."

"Ping," the bell sounds on the microwave. Fasset stirs the coffee and presents it to Greatbanks.

"OK, now let's go over whatever has brought you here. Was it the Foster and Foster report?"

Greatbanks nods his head.

"I thought so. I didn't tell Mr. Daley about it. I left that for you. Sorry! He would not have believed me anyway."

"Ping." The microwave sounds again. Fasset stirs his own cup of coffee.

"OK, so what to do now . . . did Mr. Daley say anything?"

"Between outbursts only that I had to like get the circulation numbers up."

"Yes, the Statesman is on a road to nowhere. Circulation numbers have been dropping for quite some time. It is becoming critical now. Mr. Daley is feeling the pressure, but he won't do anything to straighten the ship. He doesn't realize it, but there is less and less reason to buy the paper each day. Mr. Daley won't improve his product to keep his existing readers or to attract any new ones. There is nothing special to read in this paper anymore; what is printed by the Statesman is also available in any one of a number of alternate sources, and for far less cost, or no cost at all!"

Greatbanks nods his head as he listens to Fasset's every word.

"Greatbanks, do you remember your first day at the Statesman, our meeting with Mr. Daley? Mr. Daley had asked me to prepare a plan to increase circulation. I mentioned then that the paper should become a morning newspaper. I mentioned that it should have a presence on Capitol Hill. I mentioned that special series reporting must be returned. I mentioned an increase in sports coverage. Of those recommendations, only one has been implemented so far . . . that of becoming a morning newspaper, and that's happened only in the e-edition."

Greatbanks nods again.

"Greatbanks, don't give up now. Try to hang in there a little longer. Begin to implement what I have now just told you. Don't mention anything to Mr. Daley about your plans or our conversation. Start with Homer Dragg, over in the Editorial Department. He's your best journalist. Use him in a clandestine way, maybe with a secret byline. Begin a special series segment on something topical, maybe even political. That would be a double whammy. Initiate it now, but don't say a word to Mr. Daley. By the time he finds out, it will be too late; it will already be in motion; he won't be able to stop it; the series will have to be completed. Do this, Greatbanks, and soon, I promise you, some good things will come your way. Do not quit now, Great-banks, do not quit now!"

"Fasset, can I like call you again for guidance? Ya know, you're my only hope . . . like maybe some more ideas and how to do the special series topics?"

"Absolutely, but nothing must be mentioned about our meetings, ever! These must remain our secret."

It is agreed.

Greatbanks returns to his work station, saying nothing to any of his fellow employees about his absence. As he arrives he can see Mr. Daley in his office, bellowing something over the phone to some unfortunate soul. Greatbanks turns in another direction and picks up his phone.

"Dragg, I like need to discuss a matter with you. Please come immediately to my office."

Ten minutes later, Mr. Daley looks from his office into the newsroom. He can see Homer Dragg and Ackerley Greatbanks huddled at Greatbank's desk, and talking secretly about something . . .

Chapter Twenty

"Do you think this will work? Do you think we can pull it off?" Homer Dragg speaks softly to Greatbanks after listening to the basics of the new plan. He is really awed by it; this plan appears so intriguing and exciting to him. What a coup this could be if the plan works. Dragg is no admirer of Preston Daley at all; he would love to see Greatbanks' plan succeed, but for a different reason. Dragg was an admirer of Basil Fasset; he thought Fasset was the consummate journalism professional; he thought Fasset got a raw deal from Mr. Daley. This would be so sweet . . . to succeed in doing the very thing Basil Fasset had wanted to do, and to carry on for him, right under Mr. Daley's nose.

"Greatbanks, do you know, this is exactly what Fasset wanted. He had talked to me about it several times, but Mr. Daley wouldn't have any part of it. It was always about cost, there was no money to do a special series. Going underground with a pen name is a brilliant idea. The deed will be done before Mr. Daley even knows what happened, or by whom."

"Dragg, did you and Fasset like talk about any topics to explore? Did you like begin to work on something? Ya know, any ideas in your head right now? We want to get this off and running, like the sooner the better."

"Well, let's talk for a moment about our location here in

our nation's capitol. It is perfect. For some time I have been tracking wasteful spending by Congress, hoping that an opportunity would present itself to use it in a story. I have accumulated a large data base on the topic. Not many stories have been written about this, the media has brought little to the table with specifics, because the usual feeling around here is, 'Oh, that's just the way it is in Washington,' so everything is soon forgotten. A topic of wasteful spending by congress might be a great place to start this series, with specific names and events. That should certainly get everyone's attention, and it would most probably make a few individuals squirm. They would look bad, really, really bad. Boy, would readers be interested in a series like that . . . the more names, the better! As a bonus, the series could be reproduced in the home districts of the squirming congress people! How about that?"

"Great idea, Dragg. Like how soon can you be ready? We need at least enough material for like two or three stories per week, for a month's duration. Ya know, the series doesn't need to be like totally written on the first day of publication, but you must be able to like meet your deadlines for each installment. Ya know, can you do it?"

"Oh, you bet! I've been waiting for this opportunity. I can have the first several installments ready in five days, for Saturday's paper, then I will always be at least three installments ahead of publication."

"Perfect, but, ya know, we will like start in the Sunday Magazine Section. Then it will appear on Mondays, Saturdays, and Sundays thereafter, for like a month's duration, that's 13 installments in all. The last will appear on the final Sunday. You like have enough material, Dragg?"

"Yes, much more . . . the topic is endless."

"I almost forgot, Dragg, like what is your pen name . . . what byline will you use? Who is going to like write this series?"

"You're talking with "Allen Overt," your new underground special contributing reporter for the Statesman. Welcome him aboard!"

It's done! The Statesman will have a continuing series! Greatbanks proceeds just as Fasset had suggested; he doesn't promote anything about the series beforehand. Mr. Daley won't have a sniff; he won't become aware of it early and won't be able to interfere. The series will suddenly appear in the Sunday Magazine Section. Readers will discover it as they read the paper. Afterwards, word of mouth will take over . . . and then a full-force promotional blitz, hinting at what is likely to come in future installments. Oh, will Congress people squirm! Everyone will talk. The Statesman will have something new to offer the world, something that is in no other publication. Readers will have a reason to purchase the Statesman again!

****

Sunday,

"We the Congress . . . ."

By Allen Overt

> *"Today the Statesman begins a 13-part series documenting wasteful spending habits of Congress . . . .*
> *. . . ."*

Readers of the Statesman this morning are instantly directed to the Magazine Section. The headline on its first page, signaling what appears to be a continuing story, is neatly printed upon a parchment scroll, with the Capitol Dome in the background.

> *"The Statesman has uncovered a series of disturbing events, pointing directly at Congressional*

Members Chip Pander, Amber Plight, and Dixie Moss, tying them to an unbelievable breach of trust with the people's money."

There is no possible doubt about what will appear in the remainder of the article, and on this very first page all sub-scribers are immediately presented with something new and exciting . . . a listing of names! Highlighted are three heavy-weight Washington fixtures: a very powerful mem-ber of the House Ways and Means Committee, a long-term Congress lady from a western state, and a southern Senato-rial fixture.

Stories like this aren't supposed to appear in the Wash-ington media, of all places, and certainly not containing an accurate listing of facts! Look at Allen Overt's topics to-day . . . a wasteful construction project, a make work pro-gram, and a research grant to study the sex lives of bull frogs? What is going on here? This is so out of character. Allen Overt has pulled no punches. Who is Allen Overt? Printed in a side bar to the story is an explanation and de-scription of the 13-part series.

Statesman readers are instructed to "tune in on Mon-days, Saturdays, and Sundays for future installments." A teaser for the next installment is highlighted . . . "What costly expenditure protects grasshoppers? Discover this in installment two!"

****

This Sunday morning in his Georgetown townhouse, Preston Daley is just finishing his first cup of coffee. He calmly reaches for his newspaper; his *eyes* pop out! *"We the Congress . . ."* smacks him right in the face. *"What? Where did this come from? I didn't authorize this!"*

Ba, beep, beep, boop, boop, boop, boop! A pre-recorded vanilla message explains, "We are not presently available, leave a message after the tone."

"Greatbanks . . . call me immediately. What is the meaning of this series? Who is Allen Overt?"

Preston Daley throws his paper, which catches the edge of his coffee table. Crash, tinkle, tinkle . . . the coffee pot breaks into several pieces as it falls upon the marble floor. Bonnie hears the commotion as she walks into the library.

"Darling, what is the matter? Why are you so upset?"

Mr. Daley points at the paper on the floor.

"That!"

Bonnie picks up the paper to view, *"We the Congress"*

"Well, this looks interesting . . ."

"See here, I authorize what appears in my paper!"

Ba, beep, beep, boop, boop, boop, boop!

"Greatbanks, pick up, talk to me, talk to me, now!"

Bonnie tries to calm Mr. Daley.

"Darling, this could be a positive. My eyes were immediately drawn to it, right to it. Isn't that what you're trying to accomplish?"

Mr. Daley's phone vibrates.

"Greatbanks, what is the meaning of this? . . . . oh . . . . Roscoe, I thought you were someone else!

"Preston, *"We the Congress"* . . . brilliant . . . this new series is going to be well received. Why didn't you mention it to me last night? I've thought for some time Congress should be held accountable for its actions. It never has been in the past. It's about time. At least now someone is beginning to talk about it! Well done, Preston. Who is Allen Overt? I don't recognize the name."

Chapter Twenty One

"Like I did exactly what you told me to do . . . ya know, I was creative, ya know, I made things happen!"

What is this, an employee standing up to Mr. Daley . . . and Ackerley Greatbanks, of all people? The owner of the Statesman is somewhat taken back by this youngster's sudden brash bravado. He hadn't expected it. Mr. Daley was ready to ream Greatbanks anew, but now this! The kid is standing up for himself . . . Preston Daley is at a loss for words . . . he knows the kid may be on to something with *"We the Congress . . ."* Roscoe Blusher even confirmed this to him on Sunday, but Mr. Daley never backs down to anyone.

"Look, Greatbanks, I must approve all special features around here. That's the way it's going to be. What you've started is creative, I'll give you that; we'll see how far it goes from here. Finish the series. In the future, all special features must have my approval. Do you understand me completely, Greatbanks?"

"Yes, Mr. Daley."

"Who is Allen Overt? Where did he come from?"

"Confidentiality . . . confidentiality, Mr. Daley . . . we'll be like contracting with a number of correspondent reporters in the future; ya know, we are going to keep things fresh and interesting at the Statesman from now on."

Greatbanks walks back to his desk holding his head high. Employees in the newsroom notice something quite different about him today. All are aware of *"We the Con-*

gress . . ." from yesterday's paper, and today they can see a young man who has suddenly matured. He has a confidence about himself now that wasn't present last week. He is a new man. He is assertive. Overnight Greatbanks appears to have become a seasoned newspaper professional. How did all of that develop so fast? No one at the Statesman has a clue or even a hint that . . . the new Greatbanks is really the old Basil Fasset with chutzpah! Fasset has given Greatbanks his new courage!

❊❊❊❊❊❊❊❊❊❊❊❊❊

It didn't occur overnight, but in the third week of the series, Mr. Daley becomes aware something is happening; something special is going on at the Statesman. Allen Overt has struck a nerve. People are talking, discussing the Statesman's special series, and offering suggestions in letters to the editor about additional topics. It's been years since Mr. Daley has felt such community involvement with his paper. This is good. Mr. Daley is even receiving phone calls about it; Mr. Daley never receives phone calls!

Today Preston Daley receives the greatest news of all . . . . confirmation of a circulation increase; the printed edition's circulation has begun to increase! The numbers are not huge, only a few thousand, but an increase never-the-less, and most certainly not another decrease. Maybe Greatbanks is really on to something.

"Greatbanks, come into my office."

Greatbanks finishes his phone conversation and marches right into Mr. Daley's office.

"Yes, Mr. Daley."

"Greatbanks, we have some good news today, the Statesman increased its printed edition subscriber base. This is a positive sign. I would like to build upon this, to continue our special series features. What other ideas do you have for the future?"

What's this, "our" special series? Greatbanks' attention is quickly sparked by Mr. Daley's use of the word "our," in the phrase, "our special series features." Since when has it been "our" special series? Mr. Daley has always been against the idea. Greatbanks instantly knows . . . Mr. Daley has bought into his program completely . . . totally . . . and at 100%! His response to Mr. Daley is swift.

"Ya know, I'm so glad to hear that. Like most everything I've heard so far, comments have been like soooo positive. Like wait until you see the finish!"

Greatbanks grins noticeably. Then he answers Mr. Daley's question.

"The Redskins! Like why aren't they winning? Ya know, we need to explore that! People want to know!"

"Excellent, Greatbanks, excellent, I like that direction."

With this short conversation successfully concluded, Greatbanks walks back to his desk, and dials the scribbled number in his wallet. "Can we meet in 15 minutes?"

****

Door bell chimes ring at apartment 226 at the Vacuous Arms Apartments. "Come in, Greatbanks." Basil Fasset greets Greatbanks cordially, as Greatbanks walks into his untidy apartment. Nothing has changed in three weeks . . . dirty dishes are still in the sink and on the counter tops. Fasset's apartment is as unkempt as ever.

"Let me get you a cup of coffee."

Ping. Fasset stirs the coffee.

"I've enjoyed '*We the Congress* . . .' Publishing it solely in the printed edition was clever. How did Mr. Daley react?"

"Like not well at first, but then he calmed down. Ya know, now he is using the phrase 'our special feature,' so yes, he's like accepted it. He wants to know what's next. I think the next feature will be 'Why Can't the Redskins

Win?' Like what do you think?"

"Should work, who is going to write the series?

"That's why I'm here. Like whom should I use . . . outside . . . or in-house . . . and should we continue the unknown byline?"

"Greatbanks, absolutely continue the byline; with a correspondent reporter, some mystery is added, some depth is created, something new and exciting is added to the paper. Absolutely continue it. Contact Larry Lucre in the Sports Department. Lucre's your man to write the series!"

Fasset ponders momentarily, then volunteers, "Does Mr. Daley suspect anything? The moment you detect the slightest hint of questioning behavior, or a mood change, or a glance of the eye, or a suggestive comment, or anything strange like that, I must know quickly, I must know at once. Don't ever try to cover-up, just ignore any comment, but contact me immediately. He must never know we meet. Never! Understood?"

Greatbanks nods to Fasset.

"Agreed, now I must move quickly to meet with Lucre."

****

Larry Lucre huddles with Ackerley Greatbanks, saying little but constantly nodding his head. Then he speaks; "Greatbanks, I can do that, yes, I can do that. What is the time frame?"

"Ya know, the NFL player draft is coming up . . . I would like want to run this the four weeks preceding it, starting around the 15th. That gives you plenty of time. Can you like write 13 episodes, or is that too much?"

"Thirteen is perfect!"

"OK, like we start on Sunday the 15th. What byline will you use? Ya know, we want to keep your professional designation secure from Mr. Daley, so like what byline sounds good to you?"

"Greatbanks, I'm a football guy . . . I like intensity. How does the name, Cliff Hitts sound? It's intense, but has a nice ring to it. Cliff Hitts . . . You Know It!"

"You're right . . . like from now on you will be our correspondent reporter, Cliff Hitts! Cliff Hitts . . . You Know It!"

Chapter Twenty Two

On Saturday, the Statesman proclaims . . .

"Tomorrow's conclusion of 'We the Congress' . . . series will feature the most blatant example yet . . . of promoting waste in government for personal power and gain. This concluding segment will expose an individual caught in a most egregious act, one of using a sacred position of trust and power for personal enrichment."

It doesn't take long. Names of possible candidates begin flying around the capitol! Who is it? Who is it? What individual has the Statesman and Allen Overt compromised? Impossible to wait until tomorrow! Washington boils with anticipation!

Sunday,

"We the Congress . . . ."

By Allen Overt

"In the most blatant, egregious act yet uncovered by the Statesman's special investigation, a long term public servant, Senator Lucas Stratum, has over stepped all bounds of decency and public trust by personally enriching his own pocket to the tune

of 16 million dollars. This Senator was compensated twice for the construction of the same bridge!

Senator Stratum, via his position on the Senate's Environment and Public Works committee, was able to direct the construction contract to a company in which he is the majority owner. The $8 million dollar contract was buried deep in the education bill which passed Congress last year, but never mentioned anywhere in the bill, was the fact the bridge had already been fully funded by the state. The Senator's construction company was paid twice, by the state and the federal government, for the very same project!"

Preston Daley opens his Sunday paper. He immediately views . . . *"Senator Stratum . . . . . ?"*

Ba, beep, beep, boop, boop, boop, boop!

"We are not presently available, leave a message after the tone."

"Greatbanks, pick up, pick up now!"

****

Mr. Daley's phone rings. Just moments later it rings again. It continues ringing for most of the morning. Senator Stratum? What a bomb shell! Mr. Daley had no idea. Washington is rocking with the news. Around mid-day Mr. Daley receives a terse call from the Senator's office, demanding a recanting of the entire story and a full apology; a swift liable lawsuit is promised. Things are getting ugly.

Ba, beep, beep, boop, boop, boop, boop!

"We are not presently available, leave a message after the tone."

"Greatbanks, pick up, pick up! Call me immediately!"

A sly Greatbanks has conveniently turned off his phone.

He is spending the day in a secret hiding place, the one room apartment of Basil Fasset, a place where no one will likely find him and a place away from all the commotion. Fasset had advised Greatbanks to get away from the bomb blast that would surely follow the story, and to lay low for today to let the smoke clear away. Tomorrow will be time enough to face Mr. Daley.

Homer Dragg, protected by an Allen Overt byline, sits at home and basks in the spreading glow created by his journalistic bomb shell. Talk of the story is everywhere in the capitol, on TV, and on the radio. What an exhilarating feeling Dragg experiences today, being able to watch all the squirming and all the fall out, in total and complete anonymity. For Dragg, this series is his career achieving event, his career defining moment!

In early afternoon, Senator Stratum's office releases a statement. "The Senator has fought continually thru out his career to be the best possible steward of the people's money, and continues to do so to this day. This report is nothing more than a totally fabricated and slanderous story, ginned up by the Senator's political opposition for their personal gain. This unfortunate event is the result of an unnoticed computer glitch, and not in any way planned for any personal gain of any kind. While most unfortunate, it will be corrected immediately. The people will be made whole to the last penny!"

****

Mr. Daley is in his office early on Monday morning; Greatbanks has yet to arrive. Statesman employees buzz with conversation about Sunday's story, and can see Mr. Daley making violent gestures to someone, as he talks on the phone. Electricity saturates the newsroom! Where is Greatbanks?

Soon a mail courier rushes into Mr. Daley's office, and

hands him something requested earlier, something very important. Mr. Daley tears open the parcel; he studies its contents. What Mr. Daley is viewing this moment is stunning. He can't believe it! Where is Greatbanks?

At the far end of the newsroom the door opens, Greatbanks quietly enters. He is aware all eyes are upon him, following his every step, his every move, as he makes his way toward his desk. As he walks, a strange mood envelops him. It's a mood that he doesn't quite understand, but one that is most unnatural. It is trance like. He feels as though he is standing outside his own body, and watching himself walk across the room to his execution. Is this a sign of what is to come?

"Greatbanks, into my office!"

At Mr. Daley's command, the trance is broken; Greatbanks walks directly into Mr. Daley's office to meet his fate.

"Greatbanks, when will the Redskins series begin?"

"Like not for another three and a half weeks, ya know, on the 15th."

"We can't wait that long!"

"Like I've scheduled it for the four weeks leading up to the NFL Draft!"

"Can't wait that long!"

Mr. Daley holds up a piece of paper.

"Look, 25,000 new readers yesterday. Our special feature is working. We can't let this momentum die. Make an announcement that the Redskins series will begin this coming Sunday. Get it moving, Greatbanks! Get it moving!"

Chapter Twenty Three

"I think we should go with the story. It will give us an opportunity to put the Statesman back in its place!"

"No, no, no! Ignore it. Don't give them any free publicity. They're dying a slow death. Just let it continue!"

"Twenty five thousand papers last Sunday. We can't allow that to continue. We can get all of those lost sales back this Sunday, if we run the story! Let's stop the Statesman right in its tracks! Let's scoop them big-time on Sunday!"

At this very moment, intense discussions are taking place in the offices of the Statesman's rival newspaper, the Ledger. Top management knows what a scoop the Statesman pulled off on Sunday. The Ledger was caught completely flat-footed by the Senator Stratum story, and the Ledger's Sunday newspaper sales dropped significantly because of it. Being debated at the Ledger this morning is . . . Was this an isolated event, or is the Statesman beginning to awaken from its long slumber? Nobody knows what to expect from its new circulation manager. He is so young, with no track record at all. And then, there is the letter received just this morning.

Top management makes its decision. The Ledger will run the story on Sunday!

What story . . . what story will the ledger run this Sunday?

The Ledger will report Preston Daley's favorite painting has been stolen!

This morning the Ledger received a letter from an anonymous source, stating that a painting hanging in the home of its newspaper rival, Preston Daley, is a forgery. This was a believable tip because it is, in fact, well known that Mr. Daley has an extensive art collection. But, the confirming piece of evidence presented in the letter to validate either the original or forgery was the artist's signature. The original painting was signed "Saludo." The clever forgery was signed "Saluda!" Two photos illustrating this were attached to the letter. The thief had cleverly added a slight "tail" to the bottom of the "o" in the Saludo signature creating a barely visible "a" in the Saluda forgery. Casually noted in the letter was the opinion that no one would be able to catch this unless they were specifically looking for it. No one, other than the thief and today the Ledger, is aware of this fact. What a scoop! What a perfect way to embarrass the Statesman! What a perfect way to scoop them, literally in their own back yard!

The Ledger's plan is set in motion. During the remainder of the week, the Ledger will print a small snippet each day, hinting at a recent multimillion-dollar theft which has taken place somewhere in the city and has gone unreported. Then, on Sunday, only Ledger readers will be able to find this block-buster story in the Ledger's Magazine Section. The editors know interest in this story will be keen; something about a theft of this magnitude really grabs people's attention, but when it is disclosed that the theft is an art heist, and involves their competitor, the public won't be able to get enough of the story. Mr. Daley will be the laughing stock of the city. The Ledger will scoop the Statesman and win back its lost circulation this Sunday. Then it can follow with countless other succeeding stories, giving the topic "legs," and keeping the story alive and fresh to readers. It could be a journalistic bonanza.

On Tuesday the Ledger announces,

"Sensational event uncovered: read about it on Sunday!"

The same day the Statesman prints,

"Why aren't the Redskins winning? Our special series begins Sunday!"

The battle lines are now drawn. Mr. Daley is a fighter. He has no idea what is about to happen to him, but he will not allow the high ground to anyone. The Statesman will go "eye ball to eye ball" with the Ledger this Sunday.

On Tuesday afternoon, Greatbanks huddles with Larry Lucre. Greatbanks fidgets; he is feeling quite uneasy this afternoon about what might happen on Sunday.

"Larry, Mr. Daley is putting like incredible pressure on me. Ya know, he is moving up the beginning of the Redskins Series to this Sunday. I need a like *"Wow"* initial segment, something to *"Blast"* our readers, something to like take them away from the Ledger. The Ledger is promoting a "sensational event" for Sunday. We need to counter."

"I've already got my lead topic . . . "Football, Deer Velvet, IGF-1!"

"*That* should attract some attention!"

"You'll have my first segment by Sunday's deadline, then 12 more segments beginning on Mondays, Saturdays, and Sundays thereafter. 'When Cliff Hitts . . . You Know It!'"

****

"Greatbanks, into my office!
Mr. Daley tosses a copy of the Ledger at Greatbanks.
"This is what we're up against Sunday. The ledger is breaking a story about a $2 million theft that has gone un-

reported. You better have something to counter, and it bet-ter be good!"

"Don't worry, Mr. Daley. It will be good. Cliff Hitts is on top of this.

"Who is Cliff Hitts?"

"He's our correspondent reporter for this series. "When Cliff Hitts . . .You Know It!"

Chapter Twenty Four

A lone light shines in Mrs. Stead's second story bed-room. In the alley below her window, two figures emerge from the shadows, and carefully approach the rear door of her premises. All is quiet; there is the sound of breaking glass! The taller of the two figures reaches thru the broken window, grabs the door knob on the other side, and quickly opens the door. Now both intruders are in Mrs. Stead's back hallway, now they are in her kitchen! The shorter in-truder knocks a pot off the kitchen stove, making a terrible racket in the darkness. There can be absolutely no question that this home is in the process of being burglarized!

From upstairs, an elderly lady cries out. *"I heaaarrrrrr you, who ever you arrrrrre. Get outtttttt. I have called the poliiiiiiiice!"*

The two burglars stop in their tracks, turn, and flee the premises. Mrs. Stead is safe! Now a siren is heard ap-proaching the scene . . . flashing lights of a police car pul-sate with excitement in front of Mrs. Stead's house . . . two officers have arrived to help, but another break-in on this street in Georgetown is recorded!

Fifteen minutes later, a very flustered and most uneasy Mrs. Stead gives her report to police officers, as they ques-tion her about the attempted robbery.

"Yes officer, I am very aware of my surroundings. I

must be. You can never be too careful these days, especially with all the break-ins lately. I immediately knew what was happening. I locked my bedroom door and called 911."

"Mrs. Stead, were you able to see the thief, will you be able to identify him?"

"Oh, there were two of them. It was so dark . . . I wouldn't be able to identify them at all . . . but one is taller than the other. Does that help? I only saw them from behind as they fled down the alley . . . do you know Lieutenant Beebe? He's such a nice man. I have talked with him on the telephone."

"Yes, Mrs. Stead. Now, are you feeling comfortable enough to stay by yourself for the remainder of the night? If not, we can transport you to a hotel, if you would prefer that."

"I don't know if . . . . "

All view a man in a bath robe approaching.

"Madame, you must be terrified. I am your neighbor, Count Le Blanc, Count Pierre Le Blanc. This has to be so frightful for you, such a terrifying event for you this evening. May I be of some assistance, by offering you a room in my townhouse for the remainder of the night? You will feel perfectly safe and protected there."

How does one ever begin to explain the feelings presented at this moment? Mrs. Stead has never had the honor of meeting The Count, but she is at once disarmed by this charming, cultured, and most refined man. He is a gentleman; it is readily apparent from his very first word; instantly she is put at ease, and although having just met him, she is feeling the Count has been her life-long acquaintance and friend. Of course she will accept!

"That is so kind, Count Le Blanc, but where is Snugins, my cat Snugins? He fled outside during the break-in. Will you help me find him? Snugins . . . Here Snugins . . . Snugins!"

The officers come to Mrs. Stead's aid by shining their flash lights around the dark corners, under parked cars, into trees, all the most obvious and usual places to look for a hiding cat.

"Oh, here you are! Here you are, Snugins! Come to mother, Snugins!"

Snugins walks from behind a bush and into the arms of Mrs. Stead. She holds him lovingly, being reunited once again with her best friend in the world. Count Le Blanc approaches . . .

Hhhhsssssssssstttttttttt!

"Oh, Snugins! Snugins! Careful, Count Le Blanc, Snugins appears so terrorized by the break-in!"

"Madame, please feel most free to bring Snugins along with you. I would be so honored to be graced with not one, but two guests, this evening. Snugins is most welcome in my home."

Some twenty minutes later, Mrs. Stead, with Snugins on her lap, sits comfortably on a sofa in Count Le Blanc's parlor. The Count tries to calm her, to make her feel relaxed, to make her feel at home. They soon are talking about precautions they should always take, most anywhere in daily life. Andre enters the room, carrying a silver tray containing a pot of tea and cookies.

Hhhhsssssssssstttttttttt!

"Snugins, Snugins, Oh, you're still terrorized by the break-in. These are our friends. Settle down, Snugins. It's all OK now. These people have offered to protect us this evening."

Mrs. Stead pours a cup of tea.

"Count Le Blanc, this is so nice of you. It would have been very difficult for me to stay alone this evening. With all the burglaries lately, I have been forced to become overly cautious. I am aware of everything about me now, every little thing. I always know what is happening around me. That is how I was able to foil the robbery attempt tonight.

I heard the broken glass. I knew what was happening. I immediately called 911."

"That took great courage, Madame, to call out to the thief."

"Yes it did, but what was I to do? I wanted him to know that the police were on the way. It seemed like the correct action to take."

"Tell me, Madame, what have you seen around you? What have you observed? Is there something you have noticed that could help us all?"

"Well, no, there is nothing, other than just telling you to be alert. But, do you know, the night of the break-in across the street at Mr. Daley's home, I saw a Statesman truck on this street just before the fire truck arrived. Isn't that strange . . . a Statesman truck and then a fire engine? I told that to Lieutenant Beebe. He is such a nice man."

"What did the Lieutenant say?"

"He told me that he would keep our conversation confidential, and that every piece of evidence is important. He said they never know in advance what piece of evidence will tilt a case in their favor."

Snugins yawns, and then begins purring.

"Madame, you must be totally exhausted. Please allow me to show you to your room. You should relax now . . . I so hope you will be able to sleep soundly tonight. Snugins will be such a comfort to you." Count Le Blanc approaches Mrs. Stead.

Hhhhsssssssssstttttttttt!

Chapter Twenty Five

"Lieutenant, another robbery attempt in Georgetown last night . . . an elderly lady was nearly frightened to death. You've got to get a handle on this, and fast!"

Lieutenant Jack Beebe is standing in front of Chief Loss, feeling most uncomfortable at this moment. The Chief is becoming more vocal by the day, demanding some resolution to the events of the past year. The Chief is feeling the pressure from above, so now passes it on to his Lieutenant.

"Chief, we've put another crew down there, but we can't patrol every street every minute of the day. We're doing our best to shore up the situation, but we can't play baby sitter for the entire town. This is unlike anything we have ever experienced."

"Jack, I don't want excuses. I can't go to the mayor with excuses. The best of thieves make mistakes. You're paid to find them . . . so find them . . . and quickly!"

Lieutenant Beebe is dismissed from the Chief's office. Slowly he walks to the coffee kiosk near the entrance to headquarters, for his morning pick-me-up. Sergeant Slaytor is already there, standing in place munching on a donut.

"The Chief just chewed me out again. I'm at a loss as to what to do. What do you think, Slaytor?"

"If you're talking about last night, I don't know what to think. It kinda looks to me like someone with a butcher's knife tried to perform brain surgery. Whoever it was, he was a rank amateur, a real sloppy individual."

"Slaytor, last night's break-in was the complete antithesis of all the others. My eight-year-old nephew could have done a better job. So, are we dealing with a "me-too" imposter, or are the real thieves trying to create a diversion, trying to make us think a robbery was actually taking place?"

"I don't know. It is baffling!"

Lieutenant Beebe takes his coffee and proceeds toward his office. To the other personnel he passes while walking down the hall way, the Lieutenant appears so distant, so lost in his thoughts. No one offers to speak to him. He enters his office, and sits behind his desk thinking, I don't really want to do this, but I am going to have to speak with Mrs. Stead . . . might as well get it over with. Why are so many things happening down there on that one block in Georgetown, yet nothing happens down there at all? I just hate co-incidences. The Lieutenant picks up his phone.

"Mrs. Stead, this is Lieutenant Jack Beebe. I am most distressed to hear of the break-in at your home last night. May I come by in a few moments to talk with you?"

"Why, of course, Lieutenant, I certainly want to help in any way I can. The repairmen have just completed installing the new pane of glass in my back door. I heard the thieves break it last night . . . did you hear? You know, you can never be too careful about your surroundings, especially these days. I am very aware of everything around me. That's how I foiled their break-in. Yes, I would love to assist the police. Please come by, anytime."

Only minutes later, Lieutenant Beebe is standing at Mrs. Stead's front door. He rings the bell. The door opens before the chimes have even finished ringing . . . the strong scent of lilacs is his first greeting.

"Lieutenant, please come in, I want to do my very best to help the police."

Lieutenant Beebe takes one last breath of fresh air before entering the heavily perfumed hallway.

"What a beautiful cat you have, Mrs. Stead. What is his name? He must be of great comfort to you."

"Oh, he is. This is Snugins. He's my very best friend." Mrs. Stead holds out Snugins for Lieutenant Beebe to stroke on the forehead. Snugins begins to purr.

"Lieutenant, please come into my parlor, we can talk there."

Mrs. Stead guides the Lieutenant into a most attractive room with a floral décor, where a pot of tea and some cookies are waiting on a serving table.

"Lieutenant, please have a cup of tea with me."

Lieutenant Beebe is stuck. He doesn't want to accept this cup of tea; that will only add another 30 minutes to the interview, but what can he do? Mrs. Stead has taken the time to prepare this, so he must.

"Thank you, Mrs. Stead."

The Lieutenant gets right to business.

"I was so disturbed to hear of the break-in last night. I've already read the report, so I know what happened. Tell me, did you notice anything unusual last night?"

"Well, no, Lieutenant. It all happened so fast, but I try to be aware of my surroundings. You know, you can never be too careful these days, especially with all the break-ins lately. When I heard the breaking glass, I immediately knew. I locked my bedroom door, and called 911. The good officers were here in just minutes. I was able to completely foil the robbery!"

"What happened then?"

"Well, the officers secured my home. They were able to determine the thieves were no longer here. They then filled out their report. Oh, they offered to take me to a hotel for the night, but then my neighbor, Count Le Blanc . . . he's such a nice man, showed up and offered me a room in his townhouse, over there, for the night. Snugins and I spent the night at Count Le Blanc's townhouse. Then, this morning, the repairmen arrived to fix the broken window. That is just about everything that happened."

"I know from the report that there were two intruders. Were you able to see them? What did they look like?"

"It was too dark, but I can tell you this, that from behind, one was taller than the other. Does that help? That's all I was able to see. They were dressed in dark clothing. They ran down the alley."

"Mrs. Stead, if you can recall anything else about last night that you think would be important, please contact me. Here is my card. Call me anytime. Be vigilant! Be vigilant, Mrs. Stead!"

"Oh, I will. You can never be too alert. With all the break-ins lately, I am very aware of my surroundings. You just can't be too careful!"

Mrs. Stead guides the Lieutenant to the front door.

"You have been most helpful this morning; thank you for the tea, Mrs. Stead. Good bye, Snugins!"

Lieutenant Beebe returns to headquarters. As he enters, Sergeant Slaytor greets him in the hallway, exclaiming, "I love your new after shave . . . lilac . . . I believe?"

Chapter Twenty Six

Sunday . . .

The Ledger . . .

"Two Million Dollar Art Heist!"

"In one of the slickest thefts of recent memory, clev-er thieves have stolen a $2 million painting from a local home!"

This morning the Ledger proudly boasts to its readers . .
.

"Not even the homeowner knows!"

The Ledger has learned that a valuable painting hanging in the home of newspaper publisher Preston Daley is a total forgery! Thieves have switched paintings!" Casually mentioned further down the article is the fact that . . . *"Mr. Da-ley owns the rival Statesman newspaper!"*

Wow!!! What a story! Residents of Washington D. C. wake up this morning and are instantly spell-bound by it. This is a type of story worth reading! The Ledger has scooped the Statesman. Ledger . . . more details, more de-tails, please! This story is far more interesting reading than your usual diet of political "shenanigans." Radio and TV trumpet the story; it is being whipped into a feeding frenzy by mid-morning. At midday the art heist is all that people are talking about in the Capitol.

At his news stand in front of the Arcanum Hotel, proprietor Sid Lustrous yells out, *"Two million dollar art heist! Read all about it! Buy it here. If you don't buy it here, you don't read all about it!"*

"Sid, give me two Ledgers!" "Sid, one Ledger, please . . . Sid, a Ledger . . . Sid, why don't you have stories like this every day?"

"Read all about it! Two million dollar art heist! If you don't buy it here, you don't read all about it!"

Stack after stack of Ledger newspapers just fly off the shelves. On display innocently, and to one side of the Ledger, the rival Statesman newspaper quietly sits, and proclaims to anyone who will look, *"Football, Deer Velvet, IGF-1!"* So far, the reading public seems uninterested in the Statesman story; not many newspapers have been purchased this morning.

****

Crash! A coffee pot scatters into many pieces on the floor in Preston Daley's library; Mr. Daley is on the phone talking boisterously to someone.

"This can't be, Roscoe! This just can't be! Roscoe, get over here right now. I need your opinion. How do I counter this? Am I being scammed? Is this some hoax perpetrated by the Ledger? Do I even call the police? What do I do?"

****

Lieutenant Beebe has read the Ledger story this morning with interest. He now thinks . . . I've been vindicated! There *is* something going on in the Daley residence. That's the good news . . . now I have a crime to work with.

Now I can begin connecting the dots. Maybe I can somehow tie all the crimes together. That double false alarm at the Daley residence wasn't a double false alarm after all. But, then, there is the bad news . . . Chief Loss is going to be furious! Another burglary in Georgetown, only this time it's a sensational event; this burglary has been broadcast to the world. This is bad. This is the last thing I need now.

****

"Roscoe, how could this have happened? Is my Saludo painting a forgery? Look at it. Do you think it is a forgery? Tell me what to do!"

"Preston, the Ledger clearly states . . . and the photos clearly show . . . there is a small tail after the "o" in Saludo, making it Saluda. Now, look at your painting . . . *there* is the tail on the "o." That clearly makes it a forgery, according to the Ledger. Are they correct? I don't know. But the painting itself, no way! This is no forgery; this appears to me to be an original. . . . . *Oh, wait; oh* . . . this is a forgery! Look at the background here . . . this small section is printed, not painted . . . completely fooled me. I would never have caught it if not specifically looking for it. This is a "giclee!" These thieves are very good! Yes, very good. It's a forgery, Preston; no doubt about it now, it is a forgery, and time to call the police!

****

In early afternoon, Maxwell guides Lieutenant Beebe into the Great Room of the Daley townhouse; two sullen faces greet him. The Lieutenant quickly offers his hand to Mr. Daley . . . "Mr. and Mrs. Daley, we will get to the bottom of this, we will get to the bottom of this."

"Thank you, Lieutenant. The forgery is hanging over there."

A frowning Lieutenant Beebe walks toward the forged Saludo. He notices the occasional chair against the wall, the same chair which displayed the foot print the night of the double false alarm. He quickly scopes out the entire room. On the wall near the chair, he spies a lone smoke detector. No surveillance cameras of any kind can be seen anywhere. There is not one camera, not one, nothing at all protecting all this art work! The Lieutenant thinks, this was a robbery just waiting to happen . . . it is a wonder it didn't occur sooner.

"Tell me, Mr. Daley, how does the security system operate?"

"Lieutenant, when the system is activated, the instant any door or window is opened, 40 seconds begin to elapse. The alarm system must be disabled during those 40 seconds. If it is not disabled, central station at Horizon Security will inquire immediately as to our presence, via this speaker and that microphone, and ask our code. If they receive no response, central station will automatically sound a break-in alarm at the police station. That is their standard protocol. The police will then respond."

"OK, on the evening of the double alarm, was the system activated?"

"Of course it was! It is always activated, always! The only time the system is disabled is when we are entertaining. We certainly don't want any unsolicited police calls in the middle of that!"

"Was anyone home the night of the double alarm? Does anyone else have the pass word . . . does Maxwell have the pass word to disable the alarm system?"

"Yes he does, but the last thing we do before leaving is to make sure the system is activated. That evening Maxwell was already in the limousine, waiting for us, and he remains at the Town Club while we dine, so he could never have altered it. Besides, Maxwell has been our employee for many years. He is most trustworthy."

Lieutenant Beebe offers a rebuttal. "Please, don't take anything I ask too personally. In all our investigations, everyone and everything is suspect. We will let the evidence guide us and direct us, going forward. You would be surprised what sometimes surfaces!"

The Lieutenant glances at the Ledger photos. "You know, I am no expert at all, but I can't tell any difference between these two . . . even the picture frames are identical. Amazing . . . these thieves are very competent, very professional."

With his first physical examination completed, the Lieutenant speaks directly to Preston Daley.

"Sir, I will need to talk with you again as this investigation progresses, but for today, that is all. Thank you for being so cooperative."

Maxwell leads Lieutenant Beebe thru the foyer toward the front door; the Lieutenant notices the security control unit on the wall as he passes. After seeing it, he now can place great certainty in the fact that the security system was activated on the night in question.

Chapter Twenty Seven

"Where is the Painting Now?"

Look, the Ledger has another headline; it will not let go of yesterday's block buster story. It stirs the pot again this morning writing,

"Two million dollar painting is still missing!"

The Ledger's plan is to "tweak" their story minutely each day this week; their reading public will demand follow up stories. Follow up stories will mean many more newspaper sales. The Ledger will bury the Statesman in the process!

Preston Daley is in an especially foul mood as he arrives at the Statesman this morning. He was made the butt of many jokes yesterday. Today he is beginning to see the potential bonanza his rival will gain, at his expense. Early this morning Mr. Daley noticed the *"Where is the Painting Now"* headline in the Ledger; it's already beginning to happen; he can easily surmise the thousands of extra papers the Ledger will sell today. The Redskins series at the Statesman won't have a chance against this art heist story in the Ledger. Mr. Daley can do nothing about it. Mr. Daley always fights, but in this fight, he is totally helpless. He is at the mercy of another. He has no control. He can do absolutely nothing while his competitor slowly advances to destroy him.

At this moment, the far door of the Statesman newsroom opens. A mail courier emerges and walks toward Greatbanks' office; entering his office, he hands him something. Now the courier turns and walks to Mr. Daley's office; Mr. Daley looks up to receive his communication. All business at hand completed, the courier exits the newsroom, uttering not a single word.

Greatbanks quickly opens his dispatch and begins reading. Look at the frown developing upon his forehead. What is this? What is he reading? Where did this come from? Greatbanks finishes; he looks up and glances toward Mr. Daley's office, but Mr. Daley is still reading his dispatch. The same frown is on Mr. Daley's face, but, of course, this is nothing new. Then Mr. Daley rises and walks to his door way.

"Greatbanks!"

"Yes, I'll be right there!"

Greatbanks hustles to Mr. Daley's office, carrying his dispatch. As he enters, he can immediately sense that the usual demanding tone of his superior is absent at this meeting. Mr. Daley motions to Greatbanks, *"please be seated;"* he then sits across the table from him. Mr. Daley has seldom acted in this manner before.

Mr. Daley leans toward Greatbanks speaking in a lower tone, *"Greatbanks, I have just been delivered a very strange letter. I don't know what to make of it. It is from someone claiming to be the thief who stole my painting. He is offering me a deal . . . "*

"Mr. Daley, ya know, like I believe I have just been delivered the same letter . . . it is here."

Greatbanks presents his letter to Mr. Daley.

"Greatbanks, it is identical! What is going on here? I should inform Lieutenant Beebe of this."

The message presented in both letters is:

Sir:

You are being offered an opportunity which you have one day to accept. If you do not accept, the opportunity will be offered to the Ledger. The opportunity is spelled out below. You will be given a manuscript, which describes in detail the theft of your Virtuoso Saludo painting.

1) You will publish this manuscript immediately in the Statesman, by initiating a continuing series of its chapters.

2) Any financial gain to the Statesman, resulting from increased subscription and newspaper sales, belongs solely to the Statesman. The location of the painting is spelled out in the manuscript.

3) $10,000 will be offered to any reader who first successfully points to the location of the painting.

4) Your price, your payment for this opportunity is 500 one ounce South African Krugerrand gold pieces. The first four chapters of the manuscript will be delivered to you upon acceptance. In one week's time, the remaining chapters will be exchanged for your payment of gold. You will be given a 1-hr advance notice of the time and place to make payment. Failure to comply will void this opportunity, and the remainder of the story will be given to the Ledger.

5) Only two individuals shall ever be aware of this arrangement: yourself and your circulation manager.

6) Your acceptance of this offer will be the printed announcement in the Statesman indicating the starting date of this series.

7) You may recover your painting at your

convenience. The "giclee" is yours to keep.

Regards,

Purloin

"Greatbanks, I cannot be a part of this. This is black mail. I will not become the laughing stock of Washington. This individual must be brought to justice at once. Lieutenant Beebe needs to be informed of this immediately. He will know what to do."

"Mr. Daley . . . excuse me . . . you are like already a laughing stock in this matter, and ya know, do you want the Ledger to like profit more because of it? "

. . . . Silence! Deafening seconds of silence tick away! Nobody speaks to Mr. Daley in this manner! Mr. Daley would normally have instantly retaliated, breaking the individual into a million pieces, but this morning all is quite different. Mr. Daley is vulnerable now; he is not acting like himself anymore; he is lost, walking around in circles. He needs major assistance for the first time in his life. At this very moment, his two strongest pillars in life are being attacked; his professional and personal legs are being sawed off right from under him. Mr. Daley is feeling very unsure of himself. Mr. Daley is sinking. Mr. Daley has no strong anchor in life to save him. Mr. Daley hopelessly needs guidance . . . and here sits this kid Greatbanks, making sense.

"Greatbanks, 500 gold coins must be a great amount of money."

"Yes, but two million dollars is like even more money! Ya know, are we going to allow the Ledger to make two million dollars? Think, Mr. Daley! A week ago Sunday we like increased by 25,000 subscribers. Another 25,000 to 150,000 isn't that far away, ya know. If we like reach that level, and maintain it, like that translates to over two million dollars of increased profit. If we go beyond that, to 200,000 subscribers, that is like five million dollars of increased profit. You gotta problem with that, Mr. Daley? Ya know, can you live with five million dollars, Mr. Daley?"

Silence! The kid speaks the truth! In Mr. Daley's world, only two things are important: his art collection and making money at the Statesman. The old Mr. Daley was a fighter. He knows he needs to get back on offense. If Greatbanks is correct, he will be able to accomplish both of his goals at once, and scoop the Ledger in the process. What was unthinkable only a few moments ago now becomes the rallying flag of a new attack. Mr. Daley can see it. Now he is ready to strike, he is in motion again, he's fighting back. The old Mr. Daley is on offense once more!

"Greatbanks, we'll do it. Prepare the announcement for this afternoon's paper. I won't give the Ledger one more day of opportunity, not one! We will scoop them, and scoop them today. This story, for the Ledger, is concluded as of today. Capturing their readers will be so sweet!

Greatbanks bolts into action! The afternoon Statesman proclaims,

"Sunday, Read the True Story of the Art Heist."

Written below it is,

"Only in the Statesman will you find what really happened. The thieves will tell you how they did it in their very own words, how they stole a two million dollar painting, in 13 spell-bound segments. The location of the painting can be discovered in the manuscript; find the painting and win $10,000!"

Chapter Twenty Eight

It is late afternoon. Seargant Slator bursts into Lieutenant Beebe's office shaking a newspaper.

"Did you see this headline in the Statesman . . . *'Read the True Story of the Art Heist?'* The thieves are going to reveal how they did it, in Mr. Daley's newspaper, of all places. This is beyond all . . . what is going on?"

Lieutenant Beebe grabs the newspaper. "Let me see that. Thirteen segments with clues . . . win $10,000?"

"You better call him. This smells fishy!"

Lieutenant Beebe is already on the phone. "Preston Daley, please, this is Lieutenant Beebe calling."

"One moment, please."

"Hello, Daley here!"

"Mr. Daley, what is the meaning of this, in today's paper?"

"Lieutenant, I was going to call you. The thief contacted us. We better talk, in my office, in 15 minutes!"

"I'll be there!"

Lieutenant Beebe hangs up the phone and walks from his office. He has never experienced such an unexpected new wrinkle in any previous case. These thieves are good, always doing something unexpected. The Lieutenant is awed by their thoroughness, their creativity. They plan in detail their every move. The consequences of each move are extensively researched. They even plan exit strategies. This thoroughness is the only constant in all these cases; it is the one thing that ties them all together in his mind.

Now, more than ever, he believes the crimes in Georgetown are all related!

Lieutenant Beebe is ushered into Preston Daley's office.

"Lieutenant, please sit down."

Mr. Daley closes his door, sitting down also. He hands Lieutenant Beebe the letter.

"I received this from the thieves, just this morning. I was going to contact you, but you called first."

The Lieutenant scans the letter.

"Mr. Daley, this is black mail! The chance of recovering your painting after making a payment is quite low. Are you aware of that?"

"Yes, of course I am, but among all my options, this is clearly the best. We will catch these thieves red handed. This is your mission, Lieutenant, this is your mission. Catch the thieves when they receive the payment! This bunch will not get the best of Preston Daley!"

"Mr. Daley, how will the payment of gold be made?"

"We don't know yet, but when notified, Greatbanks will be the courier. He is the only other person besides you who is aware of this. You will tail him, and he will lead you right to the thieves. Greatbanks will not be told you will be tailing him, so therefore he should act normally, and in no way tip off the thieves."

Lieutenant Beebe frowns.

"Lieutenant Beebe, I must impress upon you the need for total secrecy. If anything leaks out ahead of time, it could . . . no . . . it will, jeopardize the entire mission. You must be standing in place for the next week with a plan in readiness, then when called upon to act you must act instantly; you must put your plan in motion instantly. You will be given only one hour's notice. That is your mission Lieutenant. For this plan to be successful, you must succeed in your mission."

Lieutenant Beebe walks from Mr. Daley's office; he has grudgingly accepted his mission. Professionally, he doesn't like it, not one bit of it. The chance for success is low, but at least he can control his end of the process. Currently this plan is not only his best option, it is his only option. He will persevere and capture these thieves, ending their reign of terror. Georgetown will be safe again. Chief Loss will be off his back.

Returning to his office, Lieutenant Beebe can't get a recurring thought from his mind. The forged painting and the original painting had exactly the same picture frame, they were exactly the same! That's been bothering him. He hadn't mentioned it to Mr. Daley, but clearly the only way to explain it would be the fact that the thief had been in the house previously. The identical picture frames point to an "inside" job. Maxwell, Mr. Daley, Mrs. Daley . . . all become his prime suspects, but each had an alibi; they were at the Town Club together the evening of the false alarms. Was there an accomplice? It's certainly possible, there could have been one; Maxwell stood to gain the most . . . until this afternoon. With the announcement in the Statesman today, Mr. Daley becomes his prime suspect. Mr. Daley would have the greatest financial benefit of all! What better way to substantially "juice" newspaper sales and then calmly retrieve one's painting!

Lieutenant Beebe decides to go over the file of the double false alarms one more time. Somewhere in that file there must be something that was overlooked, and in light of Mr. Daley becoming his number one suspect, all the more reason to search again. The Lieutenant is clearly aware how the chief chided him in their last meeting . . . "The best of thieves make mistakes . . . You're paid to find them!" He will revisit the facts again. He'll find the mistake.

Lieutenant Beebe sorts thru the stacks of folders on his desk; yes, here is the one, the file containing the Horizon Security report. As he opens it, Lieutenant Beebe reflects upon his conversation with the repairmen; they indicated to him nothing was out of order when checking the system at Mr. Daley's house the day after. But, he hasn't looked at their written report closely. Lieutenant Beebe reads the report . . . very thorough . . . the front door . . . the rear door . . . every window was examined and found to be in working order. No notation was made of any repair, or any repair needed, other than replacing the central control box. Here is something . . . a smoke detector in the great room had excessive dirt and was cleaned. Nothing else mentioned in the report.

Hmmmmmm! That's interesting. The only smoke detector in the room was above the occasional chair displaying the footprint. Here's that footprint again! The evidence is pointing toward the smoke detector and that occasional chair, but how?

And here is another confusing thought; Horizon Security sounded the burglary alarm to the police station because they detected no sounds after 40 seconds. Forty seconds for a burglary? That's some kind of record. Did the thieves know about the 40 seconds before hand? Whether they did or did not, in any event they had to know exactly where they were going. Is this another coincidence? I just hate coincidences. This is all too choreographed for me. To me, the evidence is pointing to an "inside" job!

Then what about the Statesman delivery truck? Why was it passing by at the same time? What was it doing there? Do I have to believe in yet another coincidence? This just can't be; no way. The evidence is indicating an "inside" job, and the evidence is pointing, more and more, in Mr. Daley's direction. But, something is needed to connect Mr. Daley directly. I'll need to find Mr. Daley making a mistake!

Chapter Twenty Nine

On Wednesday morning the Ledger shouts, *"Art Heist . . . an Inside Job?"*

> *"As printed yesterday in a rival newspaper, the art thief, in a most brazen act, will tell the world how he did it! That's too much for us. The Ledger will not become a part of this continuing circus, which is appearing more and more as some staged event, or at the very worst, could even be an 'inside' job. We will leave the embers of this story for our rival publication."*

Beautifully done! The Ledger has signed off on the art heist, and backhandedly poisoned the Statesman's scoop. No wonder the Ledger is number one. The Statesman is beginning to look more and more like number two.

Preston Daley is furious. Here he has scooped the Ledger big time, and what does he have to show for it? False claims the Statesman manipulated the story! His edge is gone. He can hear the steam going right out of the balloon!

"Greatbanks, come in here, now!"

Greatbanks, hearing Mr. Daley's urgency, runs to his superior.

"Yes, Mr. Daley?"

"Greatbanks, today you must counter these claims in the ledger. You must find something, anything, to neutralize

them. Make the ledger look foolish. Somehow do it! You had better do it immediately; this was all your idea, Great-banks!"

"Yes, Mr. Daley."

Back at his desk, Greatbanks goes right to the phone. He dials a scribbled number he always carries in his wallet. "Can we meet in 15 minutes . . . . . I'll be there."

****

Greatbanks arrives early at the Vacuous Arms; he rings the door bell of apartment 226. Fasset doesn't answer. Greatbanks rings the bell again. No answer, no one inside, no one appears to be at home. Why? Why would Fasset abandon him now, at precisely the moment when he needs him the most, and just 15 minutes after talking to him? A disappointed Greatbanks turns and begins walking toward the stairwell and the parking lot beyond. He hears the sound of someone rushing up the first flight of steps; the individual breathlessly appears from the stairwell; it is Fasset.

"Sorry, I had hoped to beat your arrival."

Holding a brown bag for Greatbanks to see, "I was out of coffee. With the story in the Ledger this morning, I thought you would need it. Come on in."

Fasset opens his door for both to enter. Today his apartment is an absolute pig's sty; Greatbanks detects the aroma of stale beer greeting him from within. How can anyone live like this?

"Let me fix your coffee, Greatbanks."

Fasset pulls a dirty cup from the sink. Greatbanks feels nauseous.

"Ping," Here you go, Greatbanks. Now, you need to counter the story in the Ledger, don't you?"

Greatbanks nods as he takes his coffee.

"I thought you would be calling today, so I've been

thinking about what to do. The best course of action is to accept what is thrown at you, and find a way to turn the lemons into lemonade. Turn any doubt right back upon the Ledger. Keep the high ground, but keep the controversy with the Ledger fresh. Readers will appreciate a good 'old fashioned cat fight.' Do you have any ideas about how to do this, Greatbanks?"

"No, not one, ya know that's why I've come to you."

"Greatbanks, what do we know for sure about this story? . . . We know that the Ledger somehow uncovered the story of the forgery. We know that the Ledger was totally convinced that the story was true. . . . How do we know this? Because the Ledger believed in the photos, otherwise they would not have published them and the story in the first place. And we know they were greedy, that they scooped the Statesman in a very personal way, and with a total air of superiority. . . . We also know they are out of story, but the Statesman is not."

"Fasset, like what are you saying?

"I'm saying that . . . Oh . . . there is one other thing . . . and this is pure conjecture on my part . . . the Ledger found out about the forgery from the thieves themselves! The thieves contacted the Ledger with the story, not the other way around. The Ledger did not dig up this story. It was handed to them."

Fasset turns to make his cup of coffee.

"Greatbanks, what I was about to say was, use all of this to trap the Ledger. They won't, or can't, admit that they were given the story. So let everyone believe they dug up the story, published it, and foolishly let it go when it turned out they didn't have all the facts. Remind your readers that only the Statesman has all the facts. But, the Statesman needs one more thing to become believable."

"Ping." The microwave sounds. Fasset stirs his coffee.

"Greatbanks, the Statesman needs something so powerful, so believable, that readers will instantly embrace it . . ."

"Yes, Fasset . . . like what is that?"

"The Statesman needs a block-buster statement and a reason!"

Fasset sips his coffee.

"Greatbanks, in the newspaper business, always follow the money! If you do, you will be rewarded eventually with the story's jackpot. You will have credibility; your readers will believe in you."

Fasset stares into space, thinking for a moment . . . then he speaks.

"The Statesman must simply state . . . *a valuable painting in the wrong hands is worthless!* The painting is too 'hot.' A valuable stolen painting has little value; everyone in the art world knows it is stolen. It would be far easier to ransom the painting for some fraction of its worth, and claim the prize indirectly. Readers would instantly buy such an explanation, so in framing the story this way, the Statesman would re-scoop the Ledger, and at the same time make the Ledger look foolish. It would be so obvious to everyone the Ledger didn't stay around to dig up the entire story, the Ledger didn't follow through, the Ledger didn't finish. Newspaper readers don't want to be left hanging; they want to know what happened and how! That's why they buy newspapers. *You* can say, Look, Readers, here at the Statesman we did finish the story! The Statesman finished the story, and besides, Mr. Daley wants his painting back!"

Fasset looks out the window, thinking again.

"That's the solution, Greatbanks, that's the solution!"

In the home edition on Wednesday afternoon, Statesman readers see,

"A Valuable Painting in the Wrong Hands is Worthless."

"Sunday, read how desperate thieves hope to salvage something from nothing! Read it only in the Statesman. Only the Statesman can finish this story!"

Chapter Thirty

At this moment, the far door of the Statesman newsroom opens. A mail courier emerges and walks toward Great-banks' office; entering his office, he hands him something. Now the courier turns and walks to Mr. Daley's office; Mr. Daley looks up to receive his communication. All business at hand completed, the courier exits the newsroom, uttering not a single word.

Mr. Daley tears open his envelope. It's the manuscript! Here are the first four chapters provided by the thieves, just as they said they would.

"Greatbanks!"

Greatbanks scurries to Mr. Daley. Employees in the newsroom can see something important is taking place. They can see Greatbanks rushing, carrying an envelope to Mr. Daley.

"Mr. Daley, like here we are . . . the first four chapters."

"Yes, I have my copy here. Where is my painting? Does it say here where my painting can be located?"

"Ya know, I haven't had time to read the entire manu-script yet. The thieves said the answer would like be con-tained in it. Like give me 15 minutes to find out where!"

Greatbanks returns to his desk, sits down, and begins to study the manuscript. Mr. Daley is on his phone, talking to someone. After some 15 minutes Mr. Daley is most impa-tient; he looks out and can see Greatbanks is still reading.

"Greatbanks!"

"I'll be right there, Mr. Daley."

Greatbanks makes one final stab, trying to decipher the printed words in front of him. He looks stymied. At short moment later Greatbanks appears in Mr. Daley's office.

"Mr. Daley, this manuscript does not like directly mention the location of the painting, ya know at least not in these first four chapters. I think the location is like hidden somewhere, in clues, that we must discover. Ya know, it is not obvious."

"What! What is the meaning of this? You better figure this out, Greatbanks. The deal was that the location of the painting would be in the manuscript. Now you tell me it isn't, or that it isn't obvious, whatever that means. You better figure this out, Greatbanks, you better figure this out, and fast!"

Greatbanks stumbles back to his desk. He certainly did not expect this. What to do? There is material for Sunday's initial segment, but no clue yet as to the final outcome. Not a great way to start a series. Reread these first four chapters again! Somewhere, in the manuscript, there must be the answer!

Mr. Daley picks up his phone; he dials a number from a card in his rolodex . . .

"Lieutenant Beebe, Preston Daley here. The thieves just delivered the first four chapters, moments ago . . . no, I don't know the whereabouts of my painting. The location is not mentioned anywhere in the first four chapters, unless it is in coded form, but if so we haven't discovered the key to unlocking it yet. Greatbanks is working on that at this moment. You better come right over and have a look too."

"Mr. Daley, I'll be right there."

Mr. Daley has only a brief moment to look at the manuscript before a very excited Lieutenant Beebe storms into his office.

"Mr. Daley, I'm quite anxious to see this manuscript. Have you studied it yet? Have you discovered anything?"

The Lieutenant has jumped into this new development

with gusto; it has become his main priority. At best, he knows the manuscript will at first prove to be a rather murky document, except for the fact it can be tied directly to the thieves. But that's the important part. The manuscript can tell a story. Somewhere within, the Lieutenant knows he may find an innocent "something" that might point him right in the direction of the thieves. His job, find it.

"The manuscript is here, Lieutenant," pointing to the manuscript on the table.

Lieutenant Beebe sits at the table, picks up the papers, and begins viewing Chapter One. Mr. Daley studies the Lieutenant and believes he is watching a man searching for clues as to the whereabouts of his stolen painting, but the Lieutenant is not; he is searching for a different set of clues. He carefully views the document's writing style for any tip, any tip contained in the words, words associated with a particular discipline, or ethnicity, or age range, or even printing and format. The Lieutenant at once notices that the individual who wrote this manuscript is well organized in his thoughts; the individual doesn't waste words, he doesn't bounce around randomly from one thought to another. He has a discipline about him. That is not much to go on initially, but later the Lieutenant knows he can begin his process of forming a profile of the thief.

"Mr. Daley, I would seriously doubt if there is anything contained in these first four chapters that would point to the location of your painting. Why would the thieves risk that? They are too smart. If you discovered the painting today, there would be no way for them to extract money from you next week. No, the clues will come later, if they come at all. I would like to study this manuscript in some more detail. Have you made another copy? May I take this one back to my office?"

"Greatbanks has a copy, so of course, take it with you. Maybe you can solve the riddle there!"

Later in his office, Lieutenant Beebe tries to rethink the events of the double false alarm. Lately he has never strayed from his belief that it was an inside job . . . the footprint, the 40 seconds, the Statesman truck. But how did the thieves do it? *Flash* . . . it hits him . . . it becomes so obvious to him now! Create a diversion. That's how the thieves did it. They created a diversion! They had to find a way to get in and out of Mr. Daley's townhouse without being detected. What better way than to set off a diversion? They knew they would be detected if they entered the house, so they had to camouflage themselves, to make everyone think something else occurred that night. They would disguise themselves; they would wrap themselves in a giant system failure. They knew they had 40 seconds, just enough time to cleverly switch paintings. If they didn't exceed the 40 seconds, no one would be the wiser. No one would ever be aware that a robbery occurred at all.

For Lieutenant Beebe that footprint on the occasional chair was the clue that unlocked the "how." If someone climbed on the chair with an atomizer, and sprayed smoke onto the smoke detector, the fire alarm would be set off. Sure enough, the dirty smoke detector confirmed the possibility. If it all happened within seconds of the break-in alarm, every piece of the plan would tie together nicely, and make it appear to anyone investigating that nothing more than a system failure occurred that night. Brilliant, these thieves don't disappoint! But now, knowing this, how does it help, and how does this connect to Mr. Daley?

Chapter Thirty One

"What do you think about the manuscript, Preston? Any hope the Lieutenant or Greatbanks will have success deciphering it, and locating your Saludo? . . . I agree, once reported in the art world, a stolen Saludo will be a difficult item for anyone to re-sell. Keep me posted on what happens."

Roscoe Blusher finishes his conversation with Mr. Daley. Preston is desperate. Roscoe can feel it. Preston has agreed so far to every term presented by the thief. That is so unlike him. In this matter, Preston is docile; he is obsessed with recovering his favorite Saludo. This docile behavior is not a trait Roscoe remembers. The Preston he knows always fights, but now Preston only follows; he thinks he is fighting but he is not, he is being dragged along by events. Roscoe is alarmed at his friend's new diminished mental outlook, at his current mental state. It's not a recipe for success. The Statesman will suffer eventually because of it. There is more to life than the Saludo, and Preston must realize it. That painting is completely driving his life at the moment. It's not good. Roscoe must find a way to help his dear friend. The present situation can't be allowed to continue for much longer.

This morning Roscoe sits behind his Louis XVI desk; he sips a cup of espresso as he thinks about the Saludo. Nothing is pressing today. That's the way it should be in the art world . . . leisure laced with appreciation . . . these are the prerequisites . . . they are all that matter. Maybe he'll glance at one of his art trade publications for a while . . . it's important to stay current on recent trends and developments. Roscoe picks up a newspaper from his stack. Why do his eyes stare at a particular column? He is focused on one listing, and he just stares and stares at it for a time. He is stunned! *Here is a painting for sale, Claude Gravois' "Illusions," the same painting hanging in Mr. Daley's great room!*

This can't be! Roscoe doesn't like the feel of this at all. Is he looking at another art forgery? This painting is located in a gallery in California, in San Francisco. Better contact them at once, The Galleria Serendipity. Seconds later Roscoe is on the phone and talking to Domenick Lombardi, owner and proprietor of Galleria Serendipity.

"Mr. Lombardi, I'm Roscoe Blusher of Blusher's Art Gallery in Georgetown. A troubling matter has come to my attention just this morning . . . I'm looking at the announcement of a Claude Gravois 'Illusions' for sale. Is this correct?"

"Yes it is, Mr. Blusher. It's a beautiful work. What is troubling you?"

". . . That very painting is hanging in the home of one of my clients . . . it was sold to him the first week of November . . . the painting hangs there as we speak. I am afraid I am the bearer of bad tidings, Mr. Lombardi . . . your Gravois must be a forgery."

Silence! Nothing is said! Some seconds later Roscoe detects a faint "gulp" sound, then Domenick Lombardi makes a feeble statement, "We must immediately look into this situation. Thank you for calling us, Mr. Blusher."

Afterwards Mr. Blusher doesn't feel at all good about the call. It should come as no surprise to anyone that making such a call is most distasteful. He would have hated to have been on the receiving end himself. What worries him now is the fact that suddenly, up pops another forgery. It completely fooled Domenick Lombardi, so it must be very good. Mr. Blusher has a sickening feeling that the Georgetown thieves are in some way connected with this. Better call Lieutenant Beebe at once.

Lieutenant Beebe is sorting thru files when his phone rings.

"Lieutenant Beebe, here!"

"Lieutenant, Roscoe Blusher calling. I have some information that may be of interest to you in the Daley case. This morning I became aware of a painting for sale in San Francisco, 'Illusions' by Claude Gravois . . . that is the same painting hanging in Mr. Daley's Great Room. While not directly associated with Mr. Daley's case, it appears that another forgery has surfaced in California and I would not be at all surprised if the Georgetown thieves are somehow involved. This forgery appears to be a very good one. It completely fooled a major west coast gallery. You might want to call Domenick Lombardi at The Galleria Serendipity."

"Roscoe, I hate to even ask this, but is there any chance Mr. Daley is in possession of another forgery? Are you sure his painting is an original?"

Roscoe Blusher's heart sinks. Could the thieves have switched two paintings that evening? He had never thought of such a possibility, but he didn't carefully examine the Gravois. What if? Oh, that is just too much to comprehend . . . but such a possibility must be explored now as a consequence of this morning's discovery.

"Lieutenant, I am most certain Mr. Daley is in possession of the original. There was nothing I saw that would lead me to believe otherwise."

Roscoe knows the Lieutenant does not buy his declaration. The Lieutenant's silence is a major tip off. Lieutenant Beebe certainly remembers all too well that the Saludo

forgery almost fooled him when he was specifically looking for it!

"Lieutenant, to make you feel better, I will arrange to
verify the authenticity of the Gravois, this very evening.
Would you like to be present at Mr. Daley's home with
me?"

"I will talk to Mr. Lombardi in San Francisco now. Depending upon what he conveys to me, I may or may not be
with you this evening . . . wait, no, no, I need to see this for
myself. I will be there. For sure I will be there."

This is not the way Lieutenant Beebe wanted to spend
his day. He has enough work to do with his existing cases
and doesn't need this distraction of walking off to the west
coast to inquire about problems there. But, since the question was raised, and since it involves Mr. Daley indirectly,
he must make the call.

"Galleria Serendipity, may I help you?"

"Yes, may I speak with Domenick Lombardi, please?
This is Lieutenant Jack Beebe calling from Georgetown."

"You are speaking with him. How may I help?"

"Mr. Lombardi, I have just been informed that you are
in possession of painting, "Illusions" by Claude Gravois
that might be a forge . . . ."

"Lieutenant, please allow me to correct you. Yes, we
are in possession of the painting, but I can tell you it most
certainly is not a forgery. I received a call from a Roscoe
Blusher of Blusher's Art Gallery earlier this morning sug-
gesting that we are in possession of a forged Gravois, so
that is probably your source for this inquiry. I didn't want
to provoke Mr. Blusher at that moment, and I will respond
to Mr. Blusher in writing later today informing him, but I
will tell you now that we are in possession of the original.
As unfortunate as this may be for Mr. Blusher and his client, his client must possess the forgery! The original is at
The Galleria Serendipity!"

****

Maxwell escorts Lieutenant Beebe into Mr. Daley's Great Room. Roscoe Blusher is already there, talking with Mr. and Mrs. Daley. The Lieutenant senses calmness, a sense of relief projected by the group. They cordially greet him . . .

"Lieutenant Beebe, I'm glad you were able to stop by this evening. Roscoe has informed us about the forgery in San Francisco, and I must tell you, I was most disturbed . . . to learn of the discovery of another forgery."

"Lieutenant, I am most pleased to announce to you that the painting hanging here in Mr. Daley's home is indeed the original. Come with me and I will show you why."

A mostly smiling foursome walks to the Gravois. Roscoe Blusher pulls a collapsible director's baton from his breast pocket, extends it, and begins his explanation.

"Notice, Lieutenant, the primary brush strokes lift right out of the painting toward you! Here, see what I mean? The background has less contrast, is flatter, but still has depth. In a "giclee" the background would be one dimensional, and depending upon highlighting brush strokes, the foreground would be also. Now look at the Saludo forgery. See this one tiny area, the background here . . . it is one dimensional. It is so subtle it almost fooled me initially, but there it is!"

Lieutenant Beebe nods his head in agreement. If the expert says it is so, it is so! He can't see the difference himself. For now he will acknowledge it as the truth. He certainly doesn't want to divulge his conversation with Domenick Lombardi earlier today, but how will he square the fact that two originals of the same painting exist!

Chapter Thirty Two

"Greatbanks, what have you discovered?"

Statesman employees are unaware of the contents of the letter received from the thieves, but they are aware that somehow the thieves will be directing an upcoming series about Mr. Daley's stolen Saludo, starting this Sunday. The Statesman has previously announced this. All throughout Washington a slow rumble of anticipation is building for the series, and now, today, a sense of excitement can also be felt thru out the Statesman news room. Greatbanks, however, is excited for another reason as he enters Mr. Daley's office.

"Mr. Daley, I like can't find the key to unlocking the Saludo's where-a-bouts. Ya know, I'm afraid we are like going to have to start the series without knowing the conclusion. I don't want to do this, but like I have no other options."

"Greatbanks, under normal conditions I wouldn't authorize this! It's too dangerous, but Lieutenant Beebe has speculated to me that he very much doubts the thieves would divulge the answer in the first four chapters. . . . No; they won't do that until after they have the money. I tend to agree with him, and I want my painting back. The answers will come later. Begin the series on Sunday as planned!"

****

Sunday,

The Statesman . . .

"A Valuable Painting in the Wrong Hands is Worthless . . ."

By Purloin and Allen Overt

"The Statesman today begins a testimonial by a person or persons unknown, detailing how a valuable painting was recently stolen from the home of Preston Daley, owner of the Statesman newspaper. Mr. Daley is not in any way aware of the outcome of this series. He allows its publication in the Statesman because clues are said to be contained within the manuscript, clues that can lead to the recovery of his painting. Mr. Daley's only interest is in recovering his painting!"

Wow! The Statesman has scooped the Ledger . . . Big Time!

At his news stand in front of the Arcanum Hotel, proprietor Sid Lustrous yells out, *"A valuable painting in the wrong hands is worthless! Read all about it! Buy it here. If you don't buy it here, you don't read all about it!"*

"Sid, give me two Statesmans!" "Sid, one Statesman, please" . . . "Sid, a Statesman" . . . "Sid, why don't you have stories like this every day?"

"Read all about it! A valuable painting in the wrong hands is worthless! If you don't buy it here, you don't read all about it!"

Stack after stack of Statesman newspapers just fly off the shelves. Residents of our nation's capitol are on their merry way, participating in their very own treasure hunt!

Ba, beep, beep, boop, boop, boop, boop!

"Greatbanks, here."

"Greatbanks, remind me, we must hire Allen Overt after this series is completed. We need this man on our staff at

once!"

Washington Whispers! People are beginning to talk behind the scenes! This series at the Statesman is brilliant idea. The Ledger started the story, but then fumbled the ball half way into it. The Statesman picked up the ball and is running for a touchdown. The Statesman is breaking out. Someone has gotten Mr. Daley's attention for change and this after many, many years when so many others have been unsuccessful. Today the Statesman is acting way out of character. The Statesman has been in a box for half a century, but now the sleepy newspaper that Preston Daley oversees is changing; people are beginning to notice. It is breaking out!

But, Sinister Whispers circulate also! Could this be a public relations stunt at the Statesman? If true, it certainly is a brilliant piece of marketing. Creating a treasure hunt is way over the top; what a great way to keep people focused and buying newspapers! Could this be an "inside" job? Who will benefit from increased newspaper sales? This is a last gasp effort from a failing newspaper. All of this points to an "inside" job!"

****

"Greatbanks!"

"Yes, Mr. Daley."

"Here are the circulation numbers from yesterday. Our series increased sales by 35,000 papers. Keep it moving, Greatbanks. Keep it moving!"

Greatbanks returns to his desk feeling most uneasy. He should be excited, happy with the circulation numbers, but he isn't. He is thinking ahead. He has enough material for three more segments, and then nothing. What happens at that point? What if the thieves don't provide the conclusion to the series? What if they won't divulge the location of Mr. Daley's Saludo? What if he is unable to solve the clues? Too much depends upon events not under the newspaper's control. Why should he even think the thieves can be trusted? After all they stole the painting in the first place . . . they're thieves! He doesn't like dealing with thieves! Will they even hand over the remaining chapters?

Chapter Thirty Three

The far door of the statesman newsroom opens. A courier carrying a metal attaché case emerges and walks toward Mr. Daley's office; Mr. Daley looks up, and is handed the case. With the business at hand completed, the courier exits the newsroom, uttering not a single word.

This is most unusual. What is this attaché case? Mr. Daley stares at it for a moment, not knowing what to do. He decides to open it. "Click, click," the two safety locks release; he raises the lid . . . coming into his view is an envelope containing a letter, and a key. Mr. Daley removes them and begins reading the letter.

> Sir,
>
> Your payment of gold is due. Place the gold in this case and lock it. On Friday you will be contacted again with instructions where to transport the gold, to the designated place at the designated time. Follow the instructions exactly.
>
> Regards,
>
> Purloin

Mr. Daley quickly rereads the letter . . . it's quite simple and to the point. Nothing is mentioned about his stolen Saludo or the remaining chapters, only what the thieves want . . . the payment of gold! Very short! Very direct! Mr. Daley is uneasy. This is not "give and take." This is only "take!"

"Greatbanks!"

Greatbanks rushes toward Mr. Daley's office.

"The thieves have contacted me. Sit down!"

Mr. Daley closes the door; then walks to the table, and sits across from Greatbanks. Speaking in a soft tone . . . "Greatbanks, Friday is going to be the day. The gold is to be placed in this attaché case and delivered to an unknown place at an unknown time. I don't like the looks of this. I have never liked this idea from the beginning. This was all your idea, Greatbanks; I let you talk me into it. Now I'm stuck. Greatbanks, for your sake, this better work! Greatbanks, you must be our courier in this. Greatbanks, you must appear alert and at ease at all times. Greatbanks, you must follow the instructions implicitly. Greatbanks, do you understand me on this? Greatbanks! Greatbanks! Greatbanks, do I make myself clear?"

Mr. Daley is frazzled. Greatbanks knows it. Clearly Mr. Daley is not thinking or acting normally, he just rambles on and on in his speech.

"Yes, Mr. Daley. Like do we know anything else?"

Mr. Daley hands Greatbanks the letter.

"Here it is!."

Greatbanks scans it quickly.

"Ya know, this doesn't say much, Mr. Daley!"

"Yes, I know. That's the reason I don't like it. Greatbanks, why did I ever let you talk me into this? Greatbanks, I feel like I am sending you off to pour 500 gold coins into a sewer. Greatbanks, you must follow whatever directions are given on Friday to the letter. Greatbanks, when you have the complete manuscript, and

---

know the painting's location, you may then hand over the gold, but not before. Greatbanks, make the person show you all of this before giving him the gold. Greatbanks, do you understand it? Greatbanks, do you hear me? Greatbanks, Greatbanks, Greatbanks . . . that's all."

Mr. Daley walks behind his desk. He picks up the phone and dials someone.

"Lieutenant Beebe, Friday is going to be the day. A courier just delivered an attaché case to me with a letter saying I would be contacted Friday with the drop-off location and time. Is your plan ready, Lieutenant? Can you be in place and waiting on Friday, Lieutenant? Are you confident you're ready, Lieutenant? Have you planned for every possible contingency, Lieutenant? Lieutenant . . . Lieutenant . . . Lieutenant!"

"Mr. Daley, I sense some uneasiness on your part. Are you sure you want to go thru with this?"

"I have to. We've already started the series. Besides, no one gets the best of Preston Daley. When the sun sets on Friday, I will be in possession of my painting and my gold. The thieves will have nothing. These thieves are amateurs; they will not get the best of Preston Daley. You and I will make sure of that, won't we, Lieutenant!"

". . . . . Yes . . . Mr. Daley!

Lieutenant Beebe hangs up his phone. This is it; it is time to put his plan into motion. Three teams of men will be required: one team inside the Statesman, one team outside to follow Greatbanks to the drop off location, and one team waiting at the drop off location. Once Greatbanks has the manuscript in his possession, the Lieutenant's men will swoop in to nab the thieves as they depart with the gold. They won't be able to get very far!

****

Friday, the weather turns ugly. It's been raining for

most of the night, and by morning the rain is cold, an almost icy rain, that is so typical in late winter. This is not the kind of day to walk about Washington site seeing. Mr. Daley is in his office early. Two Brinks employees have just delivered something to his office. Mr. Daley closes his door; he is totally focused on the package before him. He carefully unties the package to view its contents. Mr. Daley feels his breath being taken away . . . he is staring down, for the first time in his life, upon 500 shiny South African Krugerrand 1 oz gold pieces! It's a sight to behold.

Each coin is 32.6 mm in diameter, 2.74 mm thick, and weighs 33.93 g. The coins shine with an orange-gold luster; 8.33% of the coins' weight is in copper. The face of each coin contains a likeness of Paul Kruger, a four time President of the South African Republic. The coins look so mysterious yet elegant in their presentation. All the coins are legal tender in South Africa, worth the rand value of 1 oz of pure gold . . . and for any thief, the value in a local currency, of 1 oz of gold anywhere on earth!

Mr. Daley continues to stare at the coins before him. He is spell-bound. He fondles a few of them, turning the coins over, examining them again and again . . . letting the light bounce off them in brilliant orange-gold tones, and listening to the "jingles" created. He is captivated. Why hasn't he held gold coins before? These coins are intoxicating. These are truly pieces of art themselves. Mr. Daley is becoming at once totally infatuated and hooked on this new art form! He's becoming completely mesmerized by his coins; they are his new and legal addictive drug!

Mr. Daley can't stop staring at his gold coins. He doesn't want to part with them, but grudgingly, he knows he must, so he begins the process of letting go, letting go of his new-found treasure. Mr. Daley hesitantly reaches for the attaché case under the table. It's constructed of shiny aluminum, measuring 15" X 12" X 6" in all; it feels most substantial to him, and will easily be a safe home for his

500 gold pieces. He opens the case, and in a most embracing and loving manner, places each coin into its new home. Mr. Daley is smitten. What he now feels deep within him is attachment, and tenderness, and caring . . . all for his new treasure . . . his new golden coins!

The far door of the Statesman newsroom opens. A courier carrying an envelope emerges and walks directly to Mr. Daley's office. The eyes of two new employees in the newsroom follow his every step. The courier raps on Mr. Daley's door. Mr. Daley looks up; he instinctively closes the attaché case containing the object of his admiring eyes, and walks to open the door.

The courier hands Mr. Daley an envelope, then exits the newsroom, uttering not a single word. Four eyes in the newsroom are missing from their work stations; they have disappeared from view, following the courier.

Quickly Mr. Daley opens his dispatch. It doesn't take him long to read it.

> Sir,
>
> Attached is a key to storage locker #147 at the Smithsonian Museum of Natural History. At exactly 10:55 a.m. place the attaché case containing the gold in locker #147. You will find the manuscript there.
>
> Regards,
>
> Purloin

Mr. Daley immediately calls Lieutenant Beebe.

"I've received a note . . . storage locker #147 at the Museum of Natural History. Greatbanks will deposit the attaché case containing the gold into it at exactly 10:55 a.m. Be there!"

"We're on our way, Mr. Daley."

"Greatbanks, come here!"

"Yes, Mr. Daley?"

Mr. Daley closes the door.

"OK, Greatbanks, this is it."

Mr. Daley places the attaché case on the table. "Click, click," the case is open. Greatbanks' jaw drops! Glowing back at him are 500 brilliant Krugerrand 1 oz gold pieces. He cannot find the words to say anything.

"Greatbanks, you will carry this attaché case to the Smithsonian Museum of Natural History. Here is the key to storage locker #147. You will place the coins in that locker and retrieve the manuscript, which you will find there. Greatbanks, do not fail in this mission!"

Mr. Daley closes the attaché case, sliding the case toward Greatbanks. Greatbanks hesitates for a moment, wondering what is going to happen to him from this point. He has never seen so much money in one place in his entire life. He reaches for the case; it is very heavy; he strains as he picks it up. The case weighs more than 35 pounds!

Chapter Thirty Four

"A most nervous Greatbanks walks from the newsroom carrying Mr. Daley's precious cargo. Immediately, four eyes pick him up as he exits the building. It is only a short walk to his car, a silver 4-door sedan, and Greatbanks tries to look completely unassuming in his walk. At his vehicle, he sets the attaché case on the ground by the trunk, inserts a key, opens the trunk, picks up the attaché case, and smoothly places the case in the trunk. Greatbanks looks around as he closes the trunk, then opens the driver's door to enter, closes the door, and begins to adjust his seat belt. He starts the car, but does nothing; he is looking all around in different directions as he sits for a few moments waiting for the car to warm up. Four eyes from afar have not moved from him during this entire time.

Ready, Greatbanks' pulls his silver sedan into traffic. He is completely unaware that a very non-descript darker vehicle has begun to follow him; it remains two vehicles behind. Greatbanks innocently can see an approaching traffic light turning yellow. Not knowing he is being followed, but not wanting to be stalled in traffic, he guns his sedan to make it thru the intersection. The car behind him stops. Four eyes in the non-descript darker vehicle behind it stop and watch, as Greatbanks' silver sedan becomes smaller and smaller to them in the distance.

Greatbanks arrives at the Smithsonian Museum of Natural History without incident, and luckily finds a spot on 12th street right behind a tour bus. There is just enough space available to park. He glances at his watch. It is 10:50 a.m. He has but 5 minutes. Quickly he is out of the car, now the trunk lid is open; Greatbanks lifts the attaché case from the trunk and begins the most perilous part of his journey. This walk is extremely dangerous; he is wide open to attack from any direction. Most anything can happen. There is no possible defense of any kind. He is completely vulnerable. Greatbanks begins walking, trying not to look at all concerned as he constantly glances around him for any sign of trouble, or any sign of irregularity from any direction, but his body is shaking mightily; he is in a cold sweat; he remembers Mr. Daley's final comment, *"Greatbanks, do not fail in this mission!"*

The front door of the entrance to the Museum is just ahead of him. He has made it! Greatbanks walks inside . . . Ah, there is his destination, dead ahead . . . Restroom and Lockers! He thinks . . . not far at all, and I am on time. It is exactly 10:55 a.m.!

Greatbanks walks toward the locker storage area. Unnoticed are two men standing idly against one wall in the hallway to the left; one appears to be absorbed reading a newspaper, the other is bent over tying his shoe. Greatbanks doesn't know it, but here are Lieutenant Beebe's men, trying to look inconspicuous in an effort to blend in. His every move is being watched.

Greatbanks enters the locker area and stands before locker #147. He places his key into the lock and nervously opens the locker door. An envelope has been placed there and is waiting for him. Greatbanks opens the envelope.

Sir,

There has been a change of plans. Place your payment of gold here, then proceed to Storage Locker #111 across the street at the Museum of American History, where you will find the manuscript. This is the key.

Regards,

Purloin

What is this . . . a fork in the road? These thieves are
clever. They have presented Greatbanks with a fork in the
road! Mr. Daley had severely impressed upon him not to
turn over the gold until he had the manuscript in hand, but
the manuscript is not here, it is across the street in another
locker. Greatbanks knows if he doesn't follow the thieves'
instructions to the letter, the Statesman has lost the remainder of the story, and Mr. Daley specifically told him to follow instructions "implicitly."

So, what to do? Turn over the gold early or lose the story? He must decide. Greatbanks makes a difficult decision. He will save the story! He will deposit the gold into
this locker now and then quickly run across the street to
retrieve the manuscript. If the manuscript is there, fine; if
not he will run back and recover the gold before the thieves
have a chance to open the locker and take it.

Loud shouting echoes down the hallway leading to the
storage lockers. Hundreds of school children are entering
the hallway; the boys are screaming, running and jumping,
the girls giggling, all are making excited, boisterous noises.
The scene is reminiscent of a wild-west cattle drive. Hard
to make out individual figures . . . it's a huge moving mass
of humanity! Greatbanks slips out completely unnoticed on
his way to the locker across the street!

"Why is he taking so long?" Lieutenant Beebe's lead
officer, Aiken Lemming, wonders what is up?

"O'Rourke, walk over and see what he is doing!"

The other officer yells back to his partner . . . .

"He's gone. We've lost him!"

"I never saw him leave! Stay there. Don't let anyone escape with the gold! Is locker #147 still locked?"

"Yea!"

Several more bus loads of excited school children arrive. It's another mad house; the scene is repeating itself. Now a handsome man, casually dressed, walks from the Museum toward the storage lockers, concealed somewhat by hundreds of children running back and forth in the hallway. He walks into the locker area attracting no attention what-so-ever. Although the detectives see him, nothing registers with them because he's walking in the opposite direction. Some moments later the man emerges from the locker area carrying the aluminum attaché case. The detectives can see the man . . . but not the case . . . the case is concealed by the school children. Now they have a glimpse of the case! They will not be caught napping a second time!

"There he is! He's got the attaché case! Grab him!"

"Police! Halt! Halt at once! Police!"

The man stops on command, turns around, offering no resistance to the approaching officers as he pleasantly greets them . . . "Yes, officers?"

"You are under arrest! Hand over that attaché case at once!"

A bewildered looking man hands the case to the officers. They have their man. They have captured their thief! Work well done, the Chief will be happy! Georgetown will rejoice!

"What is the meaning of this? I have done nothing."

"Please stand against the wall!" Officer O'Rourke handcuffs the man.

Then officer Lemming grabs the case. "Click! Click!" He opens it . . . . in front of him are artist sketches of birds and animals!

"What? What have you done with the gold?"

"What are you talking about? What gold? I am an innocent man. I have no idea what this is all about. I am an artist; I am making sketches of animals and birds for a calendar; these are my working sketches!"

"Who are you? What is your name?"

"I am Gaylord Moreau. I am a graphic artist!"

"Do you have identification?"

"Yes I do. If you will be so kind as to un-cuff me, I will show you."

"Un-cuff-em, O'Rourke!"

Officer O'Rourke un-cuffs Mr. Moreau. Mr. Moreau produces a French Passport in perfect order. The officer sighs.

"Mr. Moreau, we have made a terrible mistake. We thought you were someone else. Please accept our apology."

Mr. Moreau says nothing. The officers allow their agitated suspect to proceed with his case.

"The Lieutenant isn't going to be too pleased with us. We lost Greatbanks, and now we have arrested an innocent man. Well, at least we haven't lost the gold. It's still locked in the storage locker. No one has escaped with the gold! Stay here, O'Rourke, watch the locker, and wait for further instructions!"

Chapter Thirty Five

Greatbanks walks into the Statesman newsroom carrying a bulging 3-ring notebook. He goes directly to Mr. Daley's office.

"Like here is the manuscript, Mr. Daley!"

Mr. Daley looks puzzled. He hasn't heard a word from Lieutenant Beebe. Why? Did the Lieutenant capture the thieves? What happened to his gold?

"Greatbanks, tell me what happened. Was the manuscript in the locker?"

"Well . . . yes Mr. Daley . . . well not exactly . . . well ya know, I opened the locker and this letter was like waiting for me."

Greatbanks hands the letter to Mr. Daley. Mr. Daley quickly reads its three lines.

"What, Greatbanks, you mean you handed over the gold without the manuscript?"

"Well, ya know I did like what you told me to do . . . like follow the instructions 'implicitly.' Ya know I left the gold and went to the other locker. Like sure enough, there was the manuscript! So now you have it! Like everything OK?"

"Greatbanks, you bumbling idiot!!! You left the gold alone! Where is it . . . is it still in the locker? Do you have the key?"

"Sure, right here!"

****

"I can't believe each one of you lost your man, and you, Lemming . . . you arrested an innocent man to boot!"

Lieutenant Beebe is livid as he paces back and forth in his office! Five men are lined up in front of him; they can't even look him in the eye, they stare at the floor.

"The Chief is going to have your hides for this! Then it will be my turn!"

Lieutenant Beebe's phone rings. "Yes, we lost them. An unbelievable chain of events took place . . . the gold?"

Preston Daley is anxious about his gold.

"Did the thieves make off with the gold?"

"No, that's the only good news this morning. The gold is still locked in the storage locker. I have an officer watching it."

"Well, get over there and retrieve it. Greatbanks has the key! He'll meet you in 10 minutes!"

****

Two officers and Lieutenant Beebe wait as Greatbanks walks into the Museum hallway. No one need be told that a huge amount of tension is in the air. The officers' eyes broadcast it. Greatbanks approaches the trio.

"Here's the key, locker #147, over there."

Lieutenant Beebe takes charge, taking the key from Greatbanks.

"OK, O'Rourke, close off the entrance while we do this. Lemming, give me that empty attaché case!"

Lieutenant Beebe stands before locker #147. He places the key in the lock. Will the gold be there? Will he at least salvage something today? Will Mr. Daley get his gold back? Lieutenant Beebe turns the key slowly . . . "click" . . . the door opens . . . the Lieutenant can't believe his eyes. *Nothing!* The locker is empty! How did the thieves do it? How did these thieves get the gold out?

"O'Rourke, were you here the whole time?"

"Well, yes, except for maybe a short time when I got a coffee, but no one would have been able to take it that fast!"

****

Lieutenant Beebe and Greatbanks walk into the Statesman newsroom, with Greatbanks going directly to his desk, the Lieutenant, to Mr. Daley's office. No greeting takes place as Mr. Daley firmly closes his door. Employees can sense something ugly is "going down" inside. Now Mr. Daley's arms flail around violently; his face becomes redder and redder the more he talks; his face is so red now it appears ready to burst. Mr. Daley is extremely upset. The Lieutenant just watches, and watches, and watches, but says nothing. Finished, Mr. Daley points toward the door. The Lieutenant opens it, and exits, without saying a word.

"Greatbanks, get in here!"

Greatbanks doesn't speak as he enters Mr. Daley's office.

"Greatbanks, where is my painting?"

"Like its location is contained in the manuscript, but ya know, I don't know where yet."

"I specifically gave you instructions not to hand over the gold until you knew the location of the painting. Now I am without a painting and also over a half million dollars in gold!

"You told me like to 'implicitly' follow instructions!"

"Greatbanks, this was all your idea! I never wanted any part of it in the first place! You talked me into it! You said this idea would work! Now, look at the mess you've created! You have a story you cannot finish, you have cost the newspaper over a half million dollars, and we still aren't any closer to finding my painting! Greatbanks, you are a disaster! Greatbanks, I've had all I can take of you! Greatbanks, I can't stand any more of you. Greatbanks,

you're fired! Greatbanks . . . . *get out!*

Greatbanks is stunned. He doesn't speak. He turns and walks out of Mr. Daley's office, passing his desk without stopping. Employees can see steam coming off Mr. Daley's head. The far door to the newsroom quietly opens, and then slowly begins to close. Not a sound is uttered by anyone. A transparent Greatbanks disappears for the last time behind this door, and into a harsh world which beckons him from beyond.

"Dragg, get into my office immediately!"

Statesmen employees also know that Mr. Daley needs a new circulation manager!

Chapter Thirty Six

Andre stands at Count Le Blanc's front door, talking with Maxwell.

"This last break in of the elderly Mrs. Stead's home was the tipping point. Count Le Blanc is very upset and frightened to death. We had no idea this neighborhood would be so unsafe. Now the Count fears for his life. We have no choice but to relocate; we will be moving to the Arcanum Hotel for our safety!"

Inside the Daley townhouse another conversation takes place . . . "Oh Mademoiselle, it pains me so to tell you this, but for our safety, Andre and I will be relocating to the Arcanum Hotel." Count Le Blanc pauses . . . "the Arcanum Hotel" . . . then slyly winks at Mrs. Daley.

"Oh, Count, Why? This is not at all necessary. I feel completely safe here in Georgetown, so why shouldn't you? Preston and I have lived here for many, many years . . . many happy years. We feel safer in Georgetown than in other parts of Washington or even Arlington."

"Mademoiselle, please understand . . . I am not a citizen. I am a Frenchman, with a French Passport. There are many bad people in this world. I am . . . how do you say . . . a sitting duck? I am not in my own country."

"Will . . . I . . . will we . . . ever see you again, Count?"

"Mademoiselle . . . why of course . . . the most beautiful

lady in all of Georgetown and I will never, ever part! Our lives are interconnected, and will always remain interconnected!" Count Le Blanc offers her a final "fait la baise," and then tenderly whispers, "A la prochaine, Mademoiselle!"

****

"Here it is, Maxwell, our moving van has arrived."

A small van marked "EquiPotent, Buy or Rent" pulls up in front of Count Le Blanc's townhouse.

"Bonjour, Monsieur!" . . . Andre greets one of the workmen as he steps from the van.

"EquiPotent at your service, sir. Is this the residence of Pierre Le Blanc?"

"This is my chateau," states Count Le Blanc, as he arrives from next door. We have only a few things to dispose of this morning. Please come and I will direct you to them."

Two workmen follow Andre and Count Le Blanc inside while the Count, in an apologetic manner states, "I am so very sorry to trouble you with this, but the items are on the third floor."

"For EquiPotent, no problem at all! We do it every day, sir!"

The third floor artist's studio still harbors the ever present aromas of organic inks and paints, but now appears bare, with only the two copying machines, the high end printer, and a computer remaining. The easels have been packed away.

"We can have this finished in one half hour, Mr. Le Blanc. Here, please sign our work order for release . . . and remember, in the future, for your rental needs, always call EquiPotent!"

Across the street, an elderly lady is watching and misses nothing.

Chapter Thirty Seven

This afternoon Lieutenant Beebe is at his desk doodling with his pencil, thinking about his case load of unsolved crimes. The Lieutenant has just returned from the Chief's office; the meeting wasn't pleasant. Chief Loss has been reading the newspapers too. What is this spectacle that is now taking place in his jurisdiction? Thieves are writing a *"How We Done It"* serial? Thieves have made Georgetown a national sensation and Lieutenant Beebe hasn't been able to do one thing to stop it! The Chief doesn't like this at all. He is running out of patience with his Lieutenant.

Suddenly Sergeant Slaytor rushes in with a fresh communication for Lieutenant Beebe. "Get a load of this. What do you think?" He hands Lieutenant Beebe the dispatch.

Decouvrir le pot aux roses

La pomme ne tombent pas loin de l'arbre

Lieutenant Beebe frowns. This is obviously written in a foreign language; he hasn't a clue as to what it means. Is someone trying to guide him in some way?

"Sergeant, where did this come from? Is it French, is it Italian, what is it? Do we have anyone who can translate it? Let's find out what this says, what this is all about, at once!"

"I'll get right on it."

Sergeant Slaytor takes the dispatch, and walks down the hallway. The Lieutenant continues to ponder the unsolved cases before him. He desperately needs a common thread. He has nothing to tie Mr. Daley to the crimes, but now a different thought occurs to him. What if the criminal is not Mr. Daley? So far the evidence seems to be pointing toward Mr. Daley, but it is mostly circumstantial evidence at best, nothing concrete. What if someone else is responsible? If so, who could that someone be?

The Lieutenant does not waver from his belief that the double false alarm was an "inside" job, so who could be the insider? The Lieutenant again thinks, find the "insider" and he will also solve all the other crimes. He's back to Mrs. Daley and Maxwell as prime suspects. No, he doesn't think so. What about the next layer of "insiders" . . . people who could have been in the Daley residence at some time? That could be almost anyone . . . Mr. and Mrs. Daley are a very social couple . . . they entertain often in their home. Wouldn't it be nice if they had a photographic record of their recent gatherings?

That's an idea; make a photographic record of all potential suspects! Is it feasible? Is it even possible? The idea has to be followed up. Now, let's just hope the photographs exist somewhere. Contact Mrs. Daley for help. She's the one with the answers!

Lieutenant Beebe picks up his phone and dials.

"Hello, Mrs. Daley, this is Lieutenant Beebe . . . no we haven't heard any more about the forgery in San Francisco . . . but, I have something to ask of you? By any chance have you taken any photographs of recent social gatherings in your home . . . you know, nothing formal, just casual unstructured photos of people at a party?"

"Sure we have, Lieutenant. Maxwell takes photos at all our parties. How far back do you need to go?"

"That's terrific, Mrs. Daley, I shouldn't think more than

six months for starters. Are the photos in digital form?"

"Yes they are. If you wish, I can e-mail them to you this afternoon. Why are you interested, Lieutenant?"

"Mrs. Daley, we just try to follow all the evidence and where the evidence leads us. I don't know if we will find anything here, but we try to leave no stone unturned. Every stone on every road we follow is important. Eventually we will find the correct one!"

Sergeant Slaytor breathlessly returns to the Lieutenant's office, shaking the dispatch. "I've got the answer. It's some kind of poem. Handwriting is scribbled next to the text."

Decouvrir le pot aux roses
(To uncover a secret)

La pomme ne tombent pas loin de l'arbre
The apple doesn't fall far from the tree)

"That's interesting, Slaytor. Did you determine what language?"

"French!"

"I was suspecting that. So, if this is true, I gather some-one is trying to tell us we might find something interesting around Mr. and Mrs. Daley or close to them . . . perhaps in our new layer of 'insiders.' We will wait to see what shows up when we are in possession of Mrs. Daley's pho-tos."

On this day the Lieutenant doesn't have to wait long. Mrs. Daley's photos arrive just 45 minutes later, attached to an e-mail. It states, "Lieutenant Beebe,

Here are the unturned stones you requested!"

Lieutenant Beebe can hardly wait to download the photos from the e-mail. Like a hound dog on a hunt, he is receiving new "aromas" from a different direction. He is becoming excited. He "nose" he is getting close. This is the exciting part of the chase. He bristles with anticipation. His computer screen flickers; at once all the photos jump out, brilliant and clear in front of him. He can recognize some of the faces: Mr. and Mrs. Daley, Maxwell, Senator and Mrs. Stratum, Basil Fasset, Ackerley Greatbanks, Roscoe Blusher, Chief Loss, Count Le Blanc, and then a number of faces that look familiar, but he can't attach a name. The file is marked "election evening party." There must be 50 different faces here on the various photos. He is getting closer and closer! He can feel it!

But how can he use these photos? The only person who has seen the thieves is Mrs. Stead, and she already stated she couldn't identify them, she only saw them in the dark from behind, and at some distance. So, is this another dead end? Each of these photo suspects must be interrogated and investigated individually. That's a large order.

Wait! Mrs. Humphrey has also seen the thieves . . . if the bunco cases are in any way related . . . and she has already provided us with TV look-a-likes . . . Father Knows Best and Thorny. Maybe Mrs. Humphrey will be able to recognize someone in Mrs. Daley's photos. It's at least a possibility; it's our only hope right now. We must bring Mrs. Humphrey in to look at these photos.

Lieutenant Beebe pulls the file marked "Mrs. Humphrey" from the stack on his desk. Her contact information is on the very first page; the Lieutenant dials her number . . . ring, ring, ring, ring, ring, ring, ring, ring, ring . . . she answers!

"Hello Mrs. Humphrey, this is Lieutenant Jack Beebe calling."

"Who?"

"Lieutenant Jack Beebe!"

"Who?"

"You know, the man you talked to at the police station the day you lost your money. Do you remember me now?"

"Oh, yes, have you found my money?"

"Well, not yet, but we would like to ask you to assist us in finding it. Could you come down to my office to look at some photos tomorrow? That would be very helpful to us."

"I must go out tomorrow, it is my banking day. Yes, what time should I come in?"

"How about right after lunch, say 1 p.m., can you make it then?"

"Yes, Lieutenant, I will be at the station at 1 p.m. tomorrow."

"Thank you, Mrs. Humphrey, I will be waiting for you then."

Lieutenant Beebe hangs up the phone. He must plan this meeting very carefully. He must make Mrs. Humphrey feel completely comfortable, make her feel at ease, if he expects to gain the most from the meeting. She's an older lady; she must not be stressed by anyone, and in no way be confused by too much information. Only show a portion of all the photos. Try to select photos that include all the guests, but in the fewest number of photos possible. Don't put any pressure on her.

Lieutenant Beebe's phone rings. The Lieutenant answers, "Beebe, here!"

"Lieutenant, this is Mrs. Stead. I thought you should know this; my neighbor, Count Le Blanc just moved out, fearing for his life. Did you know, the only thing moved out of the house by the movers was some office equipment from EquiPotent? Isn't that strange?"

Lieutenant Beebe sighs, why did I ever tell Mrs. Stead to be vigilant?

"Thank you, Mrs. Stead, we will check that out immediately!"

Chapter Thirty Eight

Lieutenant Beebe has not taken time for lunch. He needs every minute he has to properly prepare for this meeting with Mrs. Humphrey. All morning long he has rearranged and rearranged photos. For them to be most effective, the exact order of placement of each photo is very important; separate the small from the large group photos. Place individuals between the group photos to visually relax Mrs. Humphrey, if only momentarily; have the large group photos later in the presentation. Present no more than 10 photos in all. Any more will possibly confuse her.

Now he focuses on the meeting. No one besides Lieutenant Beebe will be present in the room during this interview. Lieutenant Beebe doesn't want any undue pressure exerted by outside influences. Have coffee, tea, and cookies available for her. Turn off the harsh daytime lighting; illuminate the two end table lights, which will cast an inviting glow when Mrs. Humphrey first enters. Make her feel at home, as if she were coming to visit in his living room. If Mrs. Humphrey has a pleasant experience, perhaps her memory will be crisper and less cluttered. All of this won't hurt. It may possibly help beyond all words. Lieutenant Beebe has but one chance to get it right, and Mrs. Humphrey is his only chance at present. A ringing phone brings the Lieutenant back to reality.

"Hello, Beebe here."

"Lieutenant Beebe, this is Mrs. Stead. You remember my cat, Snugins? Well, Snugins 'hissed' at Count Le

Blanc the night of the break in. Isn't that strange? You told me to be vigilant, so do you think Snugins was trying to tell me something that evening? He never 'hisses' at anyone, and he didn't 'hiss' at you when you were here!"

"Thanks for calling, Mrs. Stead. We'll get right on that!

This is just perfect; I can go to the Chief and tell him our primary witness is a "hissing" cat!

It's 12:45 p.m. when Sergeant Slaytor announces, "Mrs. Humphrey has arrived. Shall I bring her right in?"

Mrs. Humphrey, early? That's a good sign. "Yes, I'll see her now."

Lieutenant Beebe makes a quick glance around his office. Everything is in waiting, just as he has planned it. The cast is ready, the stage is set . . . let the play begin!

"Mrs. Humphrey, so nice of you to stop by this afternoon . . . we so want to recover your money . . . remember I promised you? You may be able to assist us in that today."

Lieutenant Beebe's warm greeting disarms Mrs. Humphrey as he guides her to the table.

"Please sit here. May I offer you a cup of coffee or tea? We also have some nice cookies. Please, join me."

The Lieutenant has not forgotten how effective this little wrinkle was when orchestrated by Mrs. Stead!

"Tea? Excellent, allow me."

Lieutenant Beebe pours a cup of tea for Mrs. Humphrey, then a cup of coffee for himself.

"Oh, this tastes so good! Mrs. Humphrey . . . I was thinking . . . perhaps somehow you could help me recover your money indirectly. . . . If we were to play a little game today . . . if I were to show you some photos . . . perhaps you might recognize someone in one of them. There is no right or wrong answer here . . . only a visual recognition on your part of anyone in the photos, and with no names required. If you don't recognize anyone in the photos, that is perfectly OK. You see . . . no right or wrong answer here . . . but every new piece of information is valuable to me. It could keep the investigation from going in a wrong direction. This should only take 5 or 10 minutes. . . . Do you think you could help me with this, Mrs. Humphrey?"

"Of course, Lieutenant, but I can't promise . . ."

"That's the beauty, Mrs. Humphrey, you don't have to!"

Lieutenant Beebe retrieves his computer from his desk, and sits down next to Mrs. Humphrey at the table. He places the computer in front of both of them. On the screen is a photo of Bonnie Daley, in her stunning blue evening dress.

"Lieutenant, this photo is so beautiful . . . so brilliant and clear. It is on your computer?"

"Yes, now days most pictures are in digital form. You can take hundreds of photos, and erase any you don't like. Then take more. It doesn't cost anything. If you want an "old fashioned" photo of a favorite, just have that one prepared. Isn't that simple? Does this lady look familiar?"

"No, I can't say she does." Mrs. Humphrey spends no time at all studying the photo.

The Lieutenant flashes the second picture, a small group photo of several ladies admiring the new Gravois painting. They are talking to a man in a blue blazer whose face is concealed.

"No . . . nothing."

The next picture is of Mr. and Mrs. Roscoe Blusher.

"No, I don't recognize them."

"You are doing fine, Mrs. Humphrey, remember there are no right or wrong answers."

Lieutenant Beebe flashes a group picture. Featured are about a dozen guests in front of the TV, watching election returns.

"No, I don't see anyone I recognize. Are you sure this is helping, Lieutenant?"

"Of course it is."

Next is a photo of Count Le Blanc and Bonnie Daley, standing in front of the bar.

"That's him, that's Father Knows Best!"

Mrs. Humphrey just blurts out her declaration!

"Are you sure, Mrs. Humphrey?"

Oh, yes, how could I ever forget? And that man behind the bar, he's Thorny!"

"*What* . . . are you absolutely sure, Mrs. Humphrey?"

The Lieutenant jumps up; he is extremely excited! With this one photo he has the evidence to solve a bunco case; with Mrs. Humphrey's testimony, he has evidence to charge Count Le Blanc and the bar tender with financial crimes today!

It is extremely difficult for Lieutenant Beebe to continue. He wants to get right up and go to the Chief's office with this new development, but there are five more photos to view. He can tell Mrs. Humphrey is relishing this little game today; she is also able to point out Count Le Blanc and the bar tender in two more photos. She is feeling most proud of herself. She likes this game. What a productive day this has turned out for Lieutenant Beebe!

"Mrs. Humphrey, I can't tell you how helpful your input has been this afternoon. Thank you for stopping in."

"When will I get my money back?"

"This all takes time, but we are getting closer to that day, Mrs. Humphrey. Thank you."

Lieutenant Beebe escorts Mrs. Humphrey from his office. Once she is outside, he turns and scurries up to Chief Loss.

"Chief, we've had a major break thru today!"

The Lieutenant briefs Chief Loss with the new developments uncovered in Mrs. Humphrey's interview.

"Chief, I think what we have here is the tip of the iceberg! If I bring Count Le Blanc in now, we run a risk . . . the risk of not being able to tie him to all the other crimes . . . and all these crimes are connected, I know it. I need a little more time to develop our case, to tie all this together. Things are beginning to unravel. Just a little more time,

Chief . . . then we can act quickly."

"Lieutenant, I need something, anything, to tell the mayor . . . now!"

"What are you going to tell him, that you have a possible suspect for *One* bunco case? That's not what he wants to hear. He wants more. Wait a short time longer, and I promise you . . . you will be able to give the mayor the *whole enchalada*!"

Chapter Thirty Nine

"Dragg, come to my office!"

Homer Dragg, the Statesman's new Circulation Manager, crisply walks into Mr. Daley's office.

"Yes sir, Mr. Daley?"

"What do you have for today's segment? Are there any clues for our readers? Better yet, are there any clues for me . . . to help me find my painting? What have you been able to find in the manuscript?"

"Mr. Daley, there was nothing in the first four segments that I was able to uncover. Today is different. We have what appears to be a clue."

"L'occasion fait le un voleur."

It's French for:

"Opportunity makes a thief."

"What has that got to do with anything? How can I find my painting with that? Isn't there anything useful, like in box #15 at the museum? Why is the clue in French?"

"I have no idea about it! The thief wrote the manuscript, not me! I . . . er Allen Overt is collaborating with the thief to make it ready for publication in the Statesman. We'll just have to follow the clues and paste them all together at the end."

"Remind me to hire this fellow, Allen Overt, when the

series is completed. We need a talent like him around here!"

"We'll see what we can do about that, Mr. Daley!" Homer Dragg chuckles to himself as he returns to his desk.

In the afternoon newspaper,

Monday,

The Statesman . . .

"A Valuable Painting in the Wrong Hands is Worthless . . .

By Purloin and Allen Overt

"L'occasion fait le un voleur."

The Statesman today asks its readers, *"Can you tell the difference? The photo on the left is the original; the photo on the right is a 'giclee.' Or is it the other way around? The clever thief has asked art experts and Mr. Daley to decide . . ."*

In today's edition, Statesman readers begin to learn about "giclees;" how they originate from a digital photo, how a sophisticated printer turns them into perfect prints, and what magic is created with highlighting brush strokes to make them paintings.

No shortages of ideas as to the locations of Mr. Daley's painting begin to surface. One very creative gentleman is even interviewed by a local TV station, saying he knows the painting is perfectly safe, and can be found at the bottom of Lake Voleur in France! It seems that all of the Washington D.C. area is becoming caught up in the hype to find Mr. Daley's painting for him.

Mr. Daley couldn't be happier, except for the fact that his painting is still missing. Circulation numbers are increasing steadily. The initial bump of 35,000 new subscribers has held. Radio and TV exposure has helped tremendously. Mr. Daley cannot remember a time when so much was commented about his newspaper by so many. It's a rather good feeling for him. Where ever he goes, common people ask him, "Any luck yet with your painting?" In a bazaar kind of way, this scene is reminiscent of the outpouring of emotions by unknown strangers, wanting to assist grieving parents in finding a "kidnapped" child. Who would have ever thought this?

****

Lieutenant Beebe continues to work on developing his case. All around him he's beginning to find new circumstantial evidence pointing directly to Count Le Blanc, but it is just that, circumstantial evidence. He can only tie one crime directly to the Count. That is not going to be enough to please the Chief. Maybe today he will follow up with Roscoe Blusher on the San Francisco forgery and see what might develop there.

"Jingle, jingle, jingle," the tiny bell sounds as Lieutenant Beebe enters Blusher's Art Gallery. Roscoe Blusher is seated behind his Louis XVI desk, drinking a cup of espresso.

"Lieutenant, what a pleasant surprise . . . any new developments?"

"No, there is nothing new in the San Francisco matter! If you don't mind, I thought today I would come in and chat with you about the art world. This is all so foreign to me. You have many beautiful paintings on display here. Could you tell me about them?"

"Why of course, Lieutenant! Why don't we walk thru the gallery as we talk? I could make you a fresh cup of coffee?"

Shortly Lieutenant Beebe sips coffee as Mr. Blusher and he approach some of the works of art in the front third of the gallery.

"Lieutenant, the pieces you see here are by popular contemporary artists. Most are oils and acrylics, but a few are water colors. I have become especially fond of water colors in recent years. Talented artists today can create "moods," or "feelings" in them not seen in older pieces. Creativity in the art world is an on-going process, always evolving."

"That area over there, is there something special about it? It looks like a gallery within a gallery."

"Yes, the alcove area contains our most valuable works; usually these are somewhat older pieces, by established artists. Let's walk over and we can see them."

The Lieutenant immediately senses this is the high rent district.

"What is back there, in the rear of the gallery?"

"Those are all our 'giclees.' They are art pieces themselves, but only as copies of an original work, and priced for the moderate purse. Don't they look elegant but functional . . . and so affordable?"

The Lieutenant can't distinguish any difference!

"Tell me, Mr. Blusher, where was the Gravois painting . . . the painting which now hangs in Mr. Daley's home . . . displayed prior to his purchase of it?"

"Oh, in the alcove area . . . it is a more valuable piece."

"My next question may be hard to answer, if there is an answer. How many people come thru your gallery on a given day?"

"That really varies, Lieutenant. On a busy weekend, there will be many visitors, maybe as many as 100 on the busiest day, but usually it's around 25 I'd guess. During the week that drops off to only a few each day. I can remember one day when not one soul stopped in!"

Lieutenant sips his remaining coffee and takes a great breath.

"You know, Mr. Blusher, I am so enjoying myself, sitting here in the gallery. I'm really beginning to appreciate the art world. I feel like these paintings are becoming my friends. They have a rather calming influence on me."

"That's an interesting comment, Lieutenant. That is exactly what Count Le Blanc said the only time he stopped in here. He said when he had time he would return and we could explore cubism together, but he never did."

"Interesting . . . tell me about that, if you can recall the details."

"Nothing to tell, really, but the reason I can recall it is that I was introduced to him socially only a few days thereafter. One thing is odd though; he spoke passionately about 20th Century art and cubism, but then went to the alcove area and showed no emotion what-so-ever when gazing upon the paintings displayed there. He just walked around in an almost robotic fashion. Strange, that is what I thought at the time."

"Was the Gravois displayed in the alcove area, the day he was here?"

"Let me think. Yes it was. That was just before the Daley's election evening party. On election evening the painting was hanging in the Daley Great Room. That evening, by the way, is the evening I was introduced socially to the Count."

Lieutenant Beebe listens but says nothing. Here is an interesting new development!

Chapter Forty

Saturday,

The Statesman . . .

> *"A Valuable Painting in the Wrong Hands is*
> *Worthless . . ."*

By Purloin and Allen Overt

> *"Ne pas voir la foret des arbres[1]*

> *"What an opportunity! A money tree is growing in*
> *Georgetown, and the fruit is just about ripe! Many*
> *valuable paintings in Mr. Daley's townhouse are*
> *waiting to be picked."*

Today Statesman readers learn of Mr. Daley's art collection and the simplistic security system in place to protect his paintings. Disbelief is the word that describes readers' first reaction. How or why didn't this crime happen sooner?

Circulation numbers at the Statesman continue to increase. Only Mr. Daley is rejoicing. Homer Dragg doesn't rejoice at all; he is becoming somewhat alarmed, for he is in possession of the total manuscript, and hasn't been able

---

[1] Can't see the trees for the forest

to determine the location of Mr. Daley's Saludo from the clues. What if he can't find the location, what to tell readers then? Dragg places his remaining clues in order,

C'est la poule qui chante qui a fait l'oeuf[2]
avoir froid, avoir chaud[3]
D'avoir ses monuments eleve[4]
à l'envers[5]
voir le bout du tunnel[6]
Il est un jeune version de son pere[7]
A sourire oreille a l'oreille[8]

Dragg hasn't the slightest idea of what to make of all this, except possibly that the last two clues might be indicating something about Mr. Daley. But, isn't that to be expected, isn't this all about Mr. Daley in the first place? And what is he going to say to Mr. Daley when he inquires again? He's got to come up with something fast. The final segment is just two weeks away!

****

Lieutenant Beebe is primed for bear! Detective work can be monotonous at times, but not now! As new devel-

---

[2] It's the chicken who sings who has laid an egg

[3] To be cold, to be hot

[4] To have one's sights set high

[5] Inside out

[6] To see at the end of the tunnel

[7] He's a younger version of his father

[8] To smile ear to ear

opments surrounding Count Le Blanc surface almost daily, the Lieutenant finds himself in a heightened state. This is the time when it is exciting to be a "cop." He's putting the final touches on his case. Even tracing down mundane leads becomes interesting, and the Lieutenant has a mundane lead at present, another loose end from Mrs. Stead to clear up. She had called a couple of days ago, commenting about Count Le Blanc's movers, the people from EquiPotent. Now, a quick visit to EquiPotent seems to be in order . . . at least see why they were moving Count Le Blanc's things.

EquiPotent's offices are located on Wisconsin Avenue, only a short drive. Lieutenant Beebe enters the office, shows his badge, and asks to speak with the manager.

"I'm the manager, Byron Smudge. And you are?"

"Lieutenant Beebe, Detective. Mr. Smudge, I am currently involved in an ongoing investigation, and I am hoping that you may be able to help me out today. A few days ago, your company removed some equipment from the home of Pierre Le Blanc. Do you recall that case?"

"Of course I do. The gentleman rented some very specialized equipment . . . equipment that we don't normally get involved with . . . it took some effort to procure it for him originally. Real high end stuff! But, he was willing to pay us well. In fact he paid the entire 6 months rental charge up front. We need more customers like him!"

"Tell me, what type of equipment are we talking about?"

"Well, computers, copiers, and printers . . . but it was the 6-color ink jet printer that was unique. We've never had any call for it previously."

"What is unusual about that printer, what is it used for?"

"Very high quality printing, commercial applications mostly, not usually for home use . . . publishers in the art world use these printers to create 'giclees' from digital photos."

"Really? Mr. Smudge, may I have a copy of the equipment rented?

"Sure, it will only take a minute. Wait here."

Mr. Smudge excuses himself to retrieve a copy. Lieutenant Beebe walks around the show room studying the various pieces of equipment. Some of these examples seem quite advanced to him . . . this new equipment, with new technology, obsoletes everything before . . . the older machines have become "Model T's."

"Here you are, Lieutenant . . . and remember, in the future, for your rental needs, always call EquiPotent!"

On the way back to the office, Lieutenant Beebe thinks about what he has now uncovered at EquiPotent. This piece of evidence about "giclees" is huge, and just think, if it weren't for Mrs. Stead it never would have turned up in the first place! It continues to add to the abundant circumstantial evidence he already has . . . every day he is getting closer and closer to a solution . . . but he doesn't yet have a direct link. He needs a direct link. The circumstantial evidence against Count Le Blanc grows stronger and stronger, but he needs that direct link to tie him to one or all the burglaries. Somewhere, Count Le Blanc has made a mistake . . . he must find it!

In his office, Lieutenant Beebe reviews his evidence. He can almost smell the fresh coat of "French" painted on each piece. The ink-jet printer for "giclees," Count Le Blanc appearing immediately after the Daley and Stead break-ins, the fact that Count Le Blanc is an "insider" at the Daleys, the 40 seconds, the stolen Statesman newspaper truck, the fact that Count Le Blanc can be traced to Blusher's Art Gallery, Mrs. Stead's hissing cat, the tip given to the police that was written in French, the clues in the Statesman written in French, the fact that Count Le Blanc can be linked socially to the set of people robbed of jewelry . . . plus the coincidence at the Museum, arresting a Frenchman. He hates all these coincidences. Then add to that Mrs. Humphrey's eye witness testimony in a bunco case against Count Le Blanc.

Today's conversation with Mr. Smudge at EquiPotent was most important. Count Le Blanc had rented the equipment for six months . . . that means his move-out date was already pre-determined by the rental contract, and not by the fact he "feared for his life." What if the Count orchestrated the failed, amateur break-in at Mrs. Stead's home in an effort to create an excuse to flee, to exit the scene without controversy? Lieutenant Beebe had originally thought the Stead robbery was different . . . that maybe the thieves had tried to create a diversion by it . . . but here would be the key piece of evidence he needs . . . to tie Count Le Blanc to that one robbery . . . the robbery at Mrs. Stead's home . . . if it could somehow be proved. **Lieutenant Beebe walks to Chief Loss' office. It is time to review developments with his superior.**

"Chief, we're getting very close. I discovered a link today between a sophisticated ink-jet printer capable of producing 'giclees' and Count Le Blanc."

The Chief at once perks up with this announcement.

"Do we have enough to finally arrest him? Can we make it stick? I don't like this wait!"

"No, presently the only thing I have for sure is a possible conviction in one bunco case with Mrs. Humphrey's testimony, plus a pile of circumstantial evidence. I will need to talk with Mr. and Mrs. Daley one more time. They may be able to add something else, such as the identity of the bar tender in the photo. I think in a couple of more days we can bring the Count in for questioning and put him in a police line-up. Then with Mrs. Humphrey's identification, we can arrest him."

Chapter Forty One

The evening meeting with Mr. and Mrs. Daley is hastily arranged. Lieutenant Beebe has no time to waste if he is going to get his man. Maxwell escorts the Lieutenant to the Daley Library where Mr. and Mrs. Daley wait anxiously for him.

"Good evening, Mr. and Mrs. Daley, thank you for meeting with me on such short notice. I feel we are making some real progress in the case, in fact, I feel we are very close to making an arrest. I need your assistance this evening on a couple of things . . . to clear up a few details."

"Lieutenant, did the photos help?"

"Yes they did, and that is one of the reasons I'm here. I have felt for some time this crime was an "inside job." The person or persons responsible knew too much; the whole crime was too well choreographed. The thieves had a prior working knowledge of what they were doing here. They knew they only had 40 seconds. For their plan to work, I believe they had to have knowledge gained by being in this house previously! There are just too many coincidences for it to be any other way."

Lieutenant Beebe opens his computer to display the photo of Bonnie and Count Le Blanc. Bonnie fidgets somewhat in her seat.

"Mrs. Daley, that's why I requested the photos; I felt that possibly there was a photo record of our thief, right under our noses. I'm very interested in this one photo . . . the bar tender in the background. Do you know this man?

How did you happen to hire him? Has he worked for you previously . . .?"

"That's Andre, Count Le Blanc's servant. The Count loaned him to us for that evening!"

"You mean this man was right next door the entire time?"

"Of course, and he has been in our home many times, as has the Count!"

"Where has Count Le Blanc moved? Do you know?"

"Ummm . . . a hotel . . . I believe. Maxwell knows for sure. I will ring for him."

Only seconds later Maxwell enters the room. "Yes, Mrs. Daley?"

"The Lieutenant has asked for the name of the Hotel that Count Le Blanc has moved to. Do you recall the name?"

"Yes, it is the Arcanum Hotel; Andre informed me the day they moved."

"Thank you, Maxwell, that is all."

"Mr. and Mrs. Daley, I must tell you, Count Le Blanc and Andre have been linked specifically to a bunco case involving an elderly lady and her missing $7,000. The only reason they have not been arrested to date is there is strong circumstantial evidence linking them to your robbery . . .

"What, Count Le Blanc?" Bonnie screams!

"Yes, and soon I will tie him to not only your case, but possibly many others too!"

Preston Daley bellows, *"Bonnie, that thief has been in our house, how many times? Bonnie, how were you fooled by such a scoundrel?"*

"I always knew there was something strange about him . . . from the very, very beginning! Something was wrong . . . I knew it . . . I always knew it! He will never be around me . . . err . . . us again! Arrest him now, Lieutenant!"

****

Early the next morning, Sergeant Slaytor walks into Lieutenant Beebe's office, casually making a snide comment.

"You have an urgent message from Mrs. Stead, call her immediately. Maybe she is out of lilac!"

"Thank you, Sergeant. I'm beginning to like lilac!"

What could she have for me now? After her last tip, she certainly deserves a quick call. Lieutenant Beebe has Mrs. Stead on the phone in seconds.

"Lieutenant Beebe, I've been thinking over and over about the events of that dreadful evening. I have recalled something now that I over looked when talking to you, which could break this case wide open; at the time I didn't think anything of it, because it came upon me so suddenly."

Lieutenant Beebe's attention is grabbed!

Yes, Mrs. Stead, what have you been able to recall?"

"Well, later that evening when I was sitting in Count Le Blanc's parlor talking about the break-in, he made a comment to me . . . 'That took great courage, Madame, to call out to the thief.'"

I replied, "Yes it did, but what was I to do? I wanted him to know that the police were on the way. It seemed like the correct action to take."

"Is that all . . . isn't there anything more, Mrs. Stead?"

"Don't you get it, Lieutenant? Only one person in the world could have known I made that comment . . . the man in my house . . . the thief. Count Le Blanc is your thief!"

Lieutenant Beebe is stunned. He had completely missed it. Mrs. Stead has just provided the missing clue, the connecting link tying Count Le Blanc to a break-in. Count Le Blanc has finally made a mistake! Mrs. Stead has solved the case! Now he has what he needs; with her written testimony he can bring in Count Le Blanc for questioning and arrest him.

"Will you come right down to the station and put that in writing, Mrs. Stead?"

"Of course I will, Lieutenant. I want to do anything I can to help out the police. You know, you can never be too careful these days, Lieutenant!"

****

The "hound dog" in Lieutenant Beebe has another scent he's picking up. Right now it's just a scent, but the man arrested by O'Rourke and Lemming at the Museum the day the gold disappeared . . . was that man either Count Le Blanc or Andre? After all, the man they arrested was French with a French Passport! Was that another diversion the thieves tried to create? He must find out about it . . . one more coincidence that must be accounted for. This one will be easy; his officers can compare the photo on his computer to the man they arrested!

"Slaytor, get Lemming and O'Rourke in here immediately!"

Officers O'Rourke and Lemming stand in front of Lieutenant, expecting to be "chewed out" one more time. Lieutenant Beebe surprises both of them with his statement; "Men, I need your input on something . . . will you look at this photo to see if you recognize anyone?" The Lieutenant turns his computer around to broadcast the photo of Count Le Blanc and Bonnie Daley to them. Instantly both respond, "That's the guy we arrested at the Museum; the bar tender is Mr. Moreau!"

"Are you absolutely certain about this?"

"Yea, we are!"

"Thanks men. You've helped me more than you will ever know. In fact, you've both just redeemed yourselves!"

It's time to go to the Chief! Lieutenant Beebe quickly rushes to Chief Loss' office, not stopping to talk to anyone on the way.

"Chief, it is time to act! As a result of our many months of tireless pursuit in this case, after many days of long, hard work, we have just obtained pieces of information that conclusively place Count Le Blanc at a break-in site, and his servant, Andre, at the gold drop off site. With this new evidence, our mountain of circumstantial evidence becomes overpowering. Tomorrow I would like to bring in both for questioning. We will place Count Le Blanc and Andre into a police line-up for Mrs. Humphrey to identify. Then we can arrest both of them at that time!"

"Why tomorrow? Why wait another day?"

"We need Mrs. Humphrey's positive identification of both of them. She's an elderly lady. Let's not risk confusing her. It's too late in the day for that now."

"Yet another day, another delay? I don't like this, Lieutenant! I don't like this at all, Lieutenant!"

****

"Hello, Mrs. Humphrey, this is Lieutenant Beebe."

"Who?"

"Lieutenant Beebe."

"Who?"

"You know, Lieutenant Beebe at the police station."

"Oh, yes, Lieutenant Beebe! Do you have my money?"

"No . . . we don't, not yet . . . but would you like to play another game with us? We will need your assistance tomorrow; we can play another game when you come in. Would you like that? Can you come to the station at 1 p.m.?"

"I must go out tomorrow, it is my banking day. Yes, what time should I come in?"

"1 p.m.!"

"I will be there, Lieutenant."

"Shall I have someone call you in the morning to remind you?"

"That's not necessary, Lieutenant, but don't call before 10:30 a.m.!"

"See you at 1 p.m., Mrs. Humphrey!"

"Slaytor, call Mrs. Humphrey at 10:30 tomorrow morning to remind her. Better yet, call her at 10:30, and then have Lemming and O'Rourke pick her up at 12:30! This is way too important. At this point in our case, we can't risk a failure!"

Chapter Forty Two

"Slaytor, get Lemming and O'Rourke in here now!"

This morning Lieutenant Beebe's plan is to bring Count Le Blanc and Andre in for questioning . . . then he will arrest both of them with Mrs. Humphrey's positive identification from a police line-up. The long nightmare of terror in Georgetown will end today.

"Lemming, O'Rourke . . . go to the Arcanum Hotel first thing and bring Count Le Blanc and Andre in for questioning. Just tell them their input is needed in an ongoing investigation. If they resist in any way, arrest them immediately on suspicion of burglary. Then at 12:30 pick up Mrs. Humphrey. We need her positive identification of both of these low-life predators."

"We'll get right on it, Lieutenant!"

Officers Lemming and O'Rourke walk out of Lieutenant Beebe's office. They pass the coffee kiosk by the entrance to headquarters, where they see Sergeant Slaytor finishing a donut.

"Let's get our coffee now, O'Rourke . . . maybe we won't have time later." Both greet Sergeant Slaytor and inform him of their mission.

"That's great, boys! Today you two will be bringing to an end a long trail of misery here in Georgetown. I can't remember anything like it in all my years on the force.

Better grab a donut too, just in case you don't have an opportunity later."

The three law enforcement officers enjoy a short respite before plunging into the day.

****

At his news stand in front of the Arcanum Hotel, proprietor Sid Lustrous yells out, *"More about the art heist! Thieves tell all! Read all about it! Buy it here. If you don't buy it here, you don't read all about it!"*

"Sid, give me two Statesmans!" "Sid, one Statesman, please" . . . "Sid, a Statesman" . . . "Sid, why don't you have stories like this every day?"

"Read all about it! Thieves tell all! If you don't buy it here, you don't read all about it!"

Stack after stack of Statesman newspapers fly off the shelves.

Officers Lemming and O'Rourke quickly pass thru all the commotion surrounding Sid Lustrous' news stand outside the hotel, and make their way thru the impressive marble entry to the main desk. Officer Lemming shows his badge to the desk clerk, asking, "In what room may I find Pierre Le Blanc?"

"One moment, sir . . . I must call the manager."

A pleasant looking gentleman dressed in a dark blue suit soon appears at the desk. "May I inquire what this is all about?"

Officer Lemming shows his badge. "We are involved in an on-going investigation, and need to speak with Pierre Le Blanc. He is a person of interest."

"I will contact him for you . . . just one moment, please . . . . It appears we have no one under that name staying in the hotel."

The officers look at each other, dumbfounded.

"Are you sure, did he ever stay here? Has he checked

out?"

"No, we have no record of him at all."

The officers stare at each other. The Lieutenant isn't going to like this.

"Wait, do you have a record of a Gaylord Moreau?"

"I'll see . . . . Yes, we do; he checked out just this morning, less than 10 minutes ago."

"Do you have a time record of the person checking out, either before or right after him?"

"One moment, please . . . . Yes, William Wilkerson and Francois Chevalier."

"That's our man, Francois Chevalier. Did he give any forwarding address or any other information?"

"I remember checking out both of them," blurts the desk clerk. "They talked in French. I couldn't tell you what they said, but they were very polite to me when speaking English."

"There they are, at the front door!"

Lemming looks up. *"Chevalier, Moreau . . . halt! Halt at once! Police!*

Now the door revolves; the suspects are outside! Lemming and O'Rourke, in hot pursuit, scramble across the marble floor after their prey. They will not lose any more suspects! Hotel guests see the officers awkwardly sliding on the marble floor as they approach the revolving door. O'Rourke's foot jams into the track. The door freezes! Lemming arrives, reverses it, and then both enter the same revolving segment in their haste to exit. Hotel patrons look at each other, in absolute disbelief at what they are viewing . . . a revolving door segment traveling forward . . . in only tiny short bursts . . . as it slowly conveys both its occupants outside the hotel. The officers are now on the street, facing all the commotion of Sid Lustrous' news stand. People are everywhere, walking in many different directions.

"O"Rourke, do you see them? Do you see them? Where are they? They have vanished!"

Lemming and O'Rourke have arrived seconds too late! They do not see a yellow cab containing Count Le Blanc and Andre, as it merges into traffic and disappears in front of them!

****

"Lieutenant Beebe, you are not going to like this at all, but Count Le Blanc and Andre have fled. We missed them by seconds . . . but we obtained names for both . . . Francois Chevalier and Gaylord Moreau."

"Great work men. Now get to work . . . check the International Flights for any record . . . also the hotels. We'll get these bad boys! They won't be able to leave the country. We'll flag their Passports! They're trapped!"

Chapter Forty Three

Reality is beginning to sink in to Mr. Daley. Sunday will be the final installment in the series and he has no conclusion to present to his readers. He has no answer, and he has no painting. Mr. Daley is furious!

"Dragg, we've been scammed by these thieves! We have no answers at all, just a bunch of worthless clues. How are we going to conclude this series? Our very credibility as a news source is at stake if we don't find an answer by tomorrow! What are you going to do, Dragg, what are you going to do?"

Homer Dragg shakes his head. "I don't know, Mr. Daley, I just don't know. Maybe something will come to me tonight."

Preston Daley focuses on fresh circulation numbers. What a bonanza for the Statesman so far! The numbers are booming! Almost 75,000 new readers have surfaced since the series began. Sunday could be the largest circulation day ever recorded in the Statesman's history . . . as readers eagerly anticipate finding the answer to the Saludo's hidden location. They won't take lightly being led into a journalistic dead end!

****

"I think we should go with the story. It will give us an opportunity to put the Statesman back in its place!"

"No, no, no! Ignore it. Don't give them any free publicity. They're dying a slow death. Just let it continue!"

"Seventy five thousand new subscribers . . . we can't allow that to continue. We can get all of those lost sales back, if we run the story! Let's stop the Statesman right in its tracks! Let's scoop them big-time on Saturday!"

At this very moment, intense discussions are taking place in the offices of the Statesman's rival newspaper, the Ledger. Top management knows what a scoop the Statesman pulled off with its *"A Valuable Painting in the Wrong Hands is Worthless"* series. This will be an opportunity to neutralize it, and at the same time tarnish the Statesman's credibility as a news source.

The topic of discussion is a letter received just this morning. The letter states,

Gentlemen,

You are being offered the opportunity to scoop the Statesman. Contained below are the published clues in *"A Valuable Painting in the Wrong Hands is Worthless"* series. Below the clues you will find the answer. Was this an" inside" job? You must decide that.

Can't see the trees for the forest

It's the chicken who sings who has laid an egg

To be cold, to be hot

To have one's sights set high

Inside out

Light at the end of the tunnel

He's a younger version of his father

To be grinning from ear to ear

The missing Saludo painting may be found in the air conditioning/heating duct directly above Mr. Preston Daley's desk!

Regards,

Purloin

Top management makes its decision. The Ledger will run the story on Saturday!

What story . . . what story will the Ledger run this Saturday?

The Ledger will publish the solution to the Statesman's series, the day before the Statesman publishes it!

Saturday . . .

The Ledger . . .

"Art Hoax? Was it an Inside Job . . .?"

"Early in this story we stated . . . 'that's too much for us. The Ledger will not become a part of this continuing circus, which is appearing more and more as some staged event, or at the very worst, could even be an inside job. We will leave the embers of this story for our rival publication.'

Today our worst fears have been confirmed.

The Ledger has learned that the missing painting has never been more than 5 feet from Mr. Daley, the Statesman's publisher, for the entire time! It can be found today, safely resting in the air conditioning/heating duct directly above Mr. Daley's desk. The last clue, 'to be grinning from ear to ear,' is most telling . . . about Mr. Daley and the Statesman."

At his news stand in front of the Arcanum Hotel, proprietor Sid Lustrous yells out, *"Read all about it! Art heist solved! "Inside" job! Buy it here. If you don't buy it here, you don't read all about it!"*

"Sid, give me two Ledgers!" "Sid, one Ledger, please" . . . "Sid, a Ledger" . . . "Sid, why don't you have stories like this every day?"

"Read all about it! Art heist solved! "Inside" job! If you don't buy it here, you don't read all about it!"

Stack after stack of Ledger newspapers fly off the shelves.

✻✻✻✻✻✻✻✻✻✻✻✻✻

Lieutenant Beebe is in possession of the same letter delivered to the Ledger. He stands anxiously in the middle of Mr. Daley's office, waiting for Officer O'Rourke to climb up the step ladder just procured from the maintenance department.

"Get up there. Be careful, O'Rourke. That's a $2 million dollar painting we're dealing with!"

"Mr. Daley, I hope that soon you will have good news . . . that you will be in possession of your painting once again!"

Mr. Daley nods at the Lieutenant. Usually Preston Daley is not at a loss for words, but here he says nothing. He is devastated by the Ledger announcement this morning.

He appears indifferent; a special reverence is required at this moment, as if the Lieutenant is about to open a tomb.

Officer O'Rourke has removed the first ceiling tile. He reaches in with his left hand, feeling around in all different directions.

"Nothing yet . . . nothing . . . nothing . . . here's something, I think I've found something over here, Lieutenant. Over here."

"OK, but be careful. What does it feel like?"

"I don't know . . . some kind of tube!"

Carefully O'Rourke pulls a metal tube from the ventilation system, and hands it to Lieutenant Beebe.

"What is it, Lieutenant? Is this the painting?"

"We'll see. Mr. Daley, let's go to the work table to properly open this." The Lieutenant notices Mr. Daley's hands are shaking.

Lieutenant Beebe and Mr. Daley sit down; the Lieutenant slowly unscrews the metal tube. He looks inside . . . something is rolled up . . . carefully, ever so carefully, Lieutenant Beebe removes a canvas . . . he un-rolls it on the table top. Mr. Daley smiles for the first time. In front of him rests his treasured Saludo painting!

"Well, there you have it, your Saludo, right above your desk! This won't help things for the newspaper, Mr. Daley. This is really going to look bad in the community, Mr. Daley."

"Lieutenant, I can assure you . . . I had nothing to do with this. I've been whitewashed!"

"No . . . no . . . Mr. Daley, you've been . . . . *Le Blanc'd!"*

Chapter Forty Four

On Sunday, the Statesman prints the only story it can possibly print . . . it apologizes to its readers!

Sunday . . .

The Statesman . . .

"Honesty and Truthfulness . . ."

This morning the Statesman gingerly approaches its readers . . .

> *"In the long history of this newspaper, our only mission has been to report events to our readers honestly and truthfully. Today we must report, with great sorrow, that we have been scammed by an unknown person, who is of interest to the police in an ongoing criminal investigation. Our source for "A Valuable Painting in the Wrong Hands is Worthless" series was not fully vetted. We didn't do our duty for our readers. It was totally our mistake. We honestly and truthfully state, to our readership and to the greater community at large, that Mr. Daley, owner of the Statesman, had no prior knowledge of events surrounding the discovery, in his office yesterday, of his stolen painting . . ."*

Will this admission work? Whether it does or does not,

the Ledger is already busy . . . actively interviewing common citizens for Monday morning's newspaper.

"Yea, I'm a little ticked off with the Statesman . . . I wanted to win the $10,000!"

"Who do they think they are, enticing us to buy their newspapers under false pretenses? I will never read another Statesman!"

"I subscribed thinking I was getting something new. I want my money back!"

At his news stand in front of the Arcanum Hotel, proprietor Sid Lustrous yells out, *"Read all about it! Art hoax! Buy it here. If you don't buy it here, you don't read all about it!"*

Very few people approach to buy newspapers.

"Read all about it! Art hoax! If you don't buy it here, you don't read all about it!"

Stacks of Statesman newspapers remain unsold on the shelves.

****

Monday morning Lieutenant Beebe huddles with his detective staff. The Chief wants an arrest, today! Count Le Blanc must be taken off the streets. The Lieutenant will not rest until he has his man!

"OK, men, until this predator is in custody, this office becomes 'Operations Central!' You will co-ordinate your efforts thru Sergeant Slaytor at each step of the process. Lemming, O'Rourke . . . your responsibility will be international air flights. Check the airports, the air lines . . . all ports of departure. You must check every flight every day until we have an arrest."

"We're on it, Lieutenant."

"Who wants hotel/motel surveillance?"

"We'll take it, Lieutenant."

"OK, now auto rental, surface transportation, ocean

shipping, and immigration. Come on men, step up."

"We'll take auto rental!"

"We've got surface transportation!"

"We'll cover ocean shipping!"

"Lemming and O'Rourke, you've also got immigration!"

"OK, Lieutenant!"

"Slaytor, have you got all this? Have you got it? You'll coordinate everyone!"

"Yea, Lieutenant, I've got it!"

Today Lieutenant Beebe places a huge "dragnet" around the city and area. It won't be long before he apprehends his man!

Chapter Forty Five

In southern Greece, two figures sit at an outdoor café and gaze over the water of the Argolic Gulf in the Peloponnese seaport town of Nafplio. It's a beautiful day, the water crystalline blue, the temperature absolutely perfect. Today this small city is the perfect place to disappear from the world; it's an ideal spot to spend some time in rest and relaxation. This wasn't always so. Nafplio, a stronghold in former times, was conquered and re-conquered thru-out its history.

"How did you know about Nafplio? No one will ever find us here!"

"Oh, there are still a few of these locations remaining in the world," replies the second gentleman.

A waiter re-fills the two glasses with ouzo. Clank, clank, a toast is given . . . "to new beginnings . . . to new opportunities . . . they are endless!" Enticing smells, from roasting goat in the charcoal pit behind them, preview the meal that is to come.

"That was a clever idea, to print the clues in French."

"Yes, it would have been interesting to see Mr. Daley's reaction . . . also Lieutenant Beebe's."

"You really had it all planned perfectly . . . . Fasset!"

"We did it together, Greatbanks. Your switch of the attaché cases in your car's trunk . . . was perfectly timed!"

"Fasset, one thing has puzzled me . . . how did you know Mr. Daley would fire me when I returned to the office?"

"After working for him for 37 years, one cannot help but know. The only important things to Mr. Daley in his life are his art collection and his money. He cares little for the feelings of other people. He really expected to recover his painting and his gold that day. You ruined it all for him. You were expendable."

"Amazing, Fasset, you knew before hand how to direct each step of this little drama."

"Yes . . . Mr. Daley and Lieutenant Beebe never had a clue. They'll be off chasing Count Le Blanc forever, I suppose, and Count Le Blanc doesn't even realize that Mr. Daley is not in possession of the gold, or that he, himself, was double crossed! But best of all, at the end of the day, everyone in Washington now thinks Mr. Daley planned the whole thing!"

Chapter Forty Six

Two years later . . .

Life is back to normal in Georgetown; the dreadful crime spree is only a distant memory. It ended as abruptly as it began. Count Le Blanc has never been heard from again; he is still missing . . .

Some changes have taken place locally.

Subscriptions at the Statesman plummeted immediately following the "Art Hoax." Mr. Daley was forced to sell what remained of his newspaper to a group of investors from New York City, who bought the Statesman via a sophisticated transaction called a leveraged buyout. Preston Daley is now retired and living alone in his mansion, with his money and his art collection. Bonnie left him for an investment banker in New York City after the sale of the Statesman.

Basil Fasset and Ackerley Greatbanks emerged after some months on holiday, and can now be found at the New Statesman working in their former jobs, as Circulation Manager and Information Technology Manager. Both are part of the all new ownership team at the New Statesman.

Joining them at the New Statesman are Homer Dragg and Larry Lucre, and popular corresponding reporters Allen Overt and Cliff Hitts.

The New Statesman is making a remarkable comeback

as a morning only e-paper, but also publishes a very limited printed morning edition which serves the central core of our nation's capitol.

Blusher's Art Gallery was acquired by the Galleria Serendipity of San Francisco. Roscoe and Honey Blusher now reside in Hawaii. Roscoe Blusher and Preston Daley are no longer speaking to one another.

Lieutenant Beebe, under intense pressure, took early retirement and was replaced by Aiken Lemming.

Mrs. Humphrey received a cashier's check for $7,000, from an anonymous, conscientious soul.

Le Blanc Chablis Gran Cru continues to be the finest white wine in the world. The winery has never heard of Count Pierre Le Blanc!

But, the most surprising news of all . . . the name Fasset turned out to be old French in origin . . . Fausette, falsehood, cheat, forgery! Fasset . . . Le Blanc'd . . . the Count!

THE END